AUDUBON'S WATCH

BOOKS BY JOHN GREGORY BROWN

Decorations in a Ruined Cemetery

The Wrecked, Blessed Body of Shelton Lafleur

Audubon's Watch

Audubon's Watch

A NOVEL

John Gregory Brown

Houghton Mifflin Company

BOSTON   NEW YORK

2001

c.1

For information about permission to reproduce selections
from this book, write to Permissions, Houghton Mifflin Company,
215 Park Avenue South, New York, New York 10003.

Visit our Web site: www.houghtonmifflinbooks.com.

Library of Congress Cataloging-in-Publication Data
Brown, John Gregory.
Audubon's watch : a novel / John Gregory Brown.
p.   cm.
ISBN 0-395-78607-X
1. Audubon, John James, 1785–1851 — Fiction.
2. Plantation life — Fiction. 3. Ornithologists — Fiction.
4. Louisiana — Fiction. 5. Artists — Fiction.
6. Death — Fiction. I. Title.
PS3552.R687 A93   2001
813'.54—dc21   2001016914

Lines from *Audubon: A Vision,* from *The Collected Poems
of Robert Penn Warren,* by Robert Penn Warren, are
reprinted by permission of Louisiana State University Press.
Copyright © 1998 by Louisiana State University Press.

Book design by Melissa Lotfy
Type is Adobe Caslon

Printed in the United States of America

QUM 10 9 8 7 6 5 4 3 2 1

To Carrie

Tell me a story.

Make it a story of great distances, and starlight.

The name of the story will be Time,
But you must not pronounce its name.

Tell me a story of deep delight.

—ROBERT PENN WARREN,
   from *Audubon: A Vision*

Acknowledgments

I would like to thank the Howard Foundation for its financial support, as well as Dean George Lenz of Sweet Briar College, who, though a physicist by training, is a poet at heart.

I would also like to thank my editor, Janet Silver, for her patience and great care; my agent, Lisa Bankoff, for her wit and wisdom; my dear friends Craig, Sheila, Julia, Eleanor, and Margot Pleasants for their festive and unflagging support; my children, Olivia, Molly, and Walker, for their boundless love and strength; and my wife, Carrie, without whom not a word of this novel could have been written and to whom its every word is dedicated.

The imagination of a boy is healthy, and the mature imagination of a man is healthy; but there is a space of life between, in which the soul is in a ferment, the character undecided, the way of life uncertain, the ambition thick-sighted.

—JOHN KEATS, preface to *Endymion*

AUDUBON'S WATCH

Prologue

"**B**eauty carries death in its arms," Emile Gautreaux, physician of New Orleans, once declared to a young apprentice while ceremoniously brandishing the scalpel with which he was about to commence the apprentice's first lesson in anatomy. This notion must have occurred at least once to the ornithologist and artist John James Audubon as he raised his rifle toward the sky and paused before taking aim on a bird whose exquisite splendor he would recreate on the page.

It was indeed beauty and death that brought these two men together. On July 31, 1821, at the estate of James and Lucretia Pirrie in St. Francisville, Louisiana, where Audubon was employed as a tutor to the Pirries' charming, coquettish daughter and to which Gautreaux had traveled in order to meet the man whose drawings he so admired, the two men spent the night not engaged in pleasant conversation, as Gautreaux had hoped, but keeping watch over the body of Gautreaux's wife.

Myra Richardson's striking beauty and curiously frank manner had enchanted and tormented a variety of men before her marriage to Emile Gautreaux. And throughout his life Audubon made gifts of his drawings to women who excited his interest, with coy and affectionate tributes hastily scrawled in charcoal pencil on the back. But the manner of Myra Gautreaux's death — its mystery and vulgarity, its suggestion of exaltation, its intimation of despair — and the troubling beauty of even her lifeless body seemed to assure that both men would never free themselves from their memory of this evening.

Thirty years later, confined to his bed and amid his mind's ceaseless wanderings, Audubon turned again to his meeting with Emile Gautreaux. He spoke not to his sons, John Woodhouse and Victor, nor to his wife, Lucy, nor to his dear friend, John Bachman, but to his two daughters, grown in his mind's eye to their full grace and beauty.

Just as Audubon finally spoke, so did Emile Gautreaux. His carriage made its way from New Orleans to New York, an arduous journey lasting nearly a month. But what was a month? It was nothing. For thirty years passion and grief had burrowed so deep that they had invaded every chalky bone to the marrow. They had feasted with insatiable appetite on the soul. They had become both sustainer and destroyer, mother and infant, victor and victim, carrion and cathedral, the earth's lime and loam. Here was the very embrace of the heavens.

Audubon's Letter

They believe, my dear young Lucy, my dear sweet Rose, that my noble mind is in ruins, that my wits have been dulled. Yes, I have demanded, despite the cold, that the room's windows remain open, but I have done so only that I might hear the voices of the rivermen on the Hudson, their throaty laughter, their musical curses, their mocking shouts. If the wind turns eastward, I will smell not merely the river's muddy shore but the ocean's brine. Westward, and I will detect, despite the chill, my orchard's pungent offerings: pears and plums and apples, quince and apricot and peaches, all left to rot, month after month, where they have fallen.

The oaks and chestnuts are bare. Their branches are transformed into dark and bony fingers against the sky. If I possessed sufficient faith, my dear sweet girls, I believe I might wake in the middle of the night and see, beyond these branches, beyond even the shimmering stars, the great unblinking eye that watches over us, that allows my steady, irreversible decline. I would join the rivermen in their labor, feed coals to the whistling engines, wade into the rushing western rivers, ascend the steepest and most treacherous summits. I would traverse this country a thousand times more to be sure that I have found them all. I cannot have found them all.

You do not understand, I know. I will tell you a story, then, about my childish nature, about how difficult it is to put failures of character aside. I once purchased a useless timepiece, a watch, but made good use of it nevertheless, just as my childhood's whimsical fascinations became the seed from which my life's work sprouted. My aim here is, as always, a modest one, that I might instruct you to some small degree, my cherished daughters, in the great complexity of our frail race.

As a boy, I had no use for mathematics, though I swore to my father each time he set sail full allegiance and devotion to my studies. Though pen and tablet lay before me, my imagination took aim not upon differences and sums but upon my father's — your grandfather's — estimable figure. I imagined him standing at full attention upon the rolling deck of the *Cerbère,* ordering his men about while his own feet remained planted on the deck as if they were a tree's roots embedded in the earth. In my mind's eye, my father kept his sights trained on the shimmering horizon as he awaited the appearance, as if from out a dream, of the British corsair or privateer whose proximity he alone sensed. I imagined the ensuing battle, my father bleeding from his arm or thigh — I would touch these wounds, my daughters, as though they were our Savior's. My father shouted out so that he must be obeyed, demanding that the ship's physician attend to those whose injuries were of greater consequence than his own.

Frightened by my imagination's constructs, I escaped outdoors, the parrot Mignonne clutching my shoulder and spreading her clipped wings in memory of flight. Have I spoken before of Mignonne, of her exotic beauty? No matter; she was the first of thousands I adored. I raced down to the wooded banks of the Loire, my arms outstretched, my hair cascading down my back, lifted by the rush of wind. I ignored the protests of my helpless tutor, a young Jesuit, who stood in the doorway, stomped his dark polished boots, and shouted, "Jean-Jacques, consider your father's wishes! There will be consequences, my young friend!"

Yes, there were consequences, for numbers have indeed always bedeviled me, tricked me like a pickpocket, led me to ruin — and here you must forgive my coarse tongue — like a whore. With such a marked deficiency in my education, I would not have thought to note when I acquired the watch of which I speak that I had been sent abroad by my father precisely half my lifetime ago. I had been eighteen and was now thirty-six. I had been a citizen of one country but now belonged to another, a Frenchman transformed into an American.

And my life, which had once seemed incalculable, immeasurable, was now — though this, of course, I could not have known — more than half done. Just as now, as you must discern, it has about reached its end. Am I not again bedeviled by numbers?

The watch? Yes, I promised to tell you of the watch. Well, I acquired it for three dollars, though I had not a penny to spare, aboard the flatboat that took me to New Orleans, away from your mother and brothers in Cincinnati. The water was low and utterly still and as brown as dark ale when my companions and I prepared to set off. Our provisions were crated, our rifles were slung across our backs, our manner was both resolute and gay, as is the custom of men who would leave behind the comforts and consolations of home.

Your mother stood silently on the muddy shore, clasping the hands of young John and Victor as though she feared that once all aboard the flatboat was secured, I might draw them to me with the promise of a warm embrace and lure them away on this adventure. I stepped off the boat and stood before her, smiling at the boys, touching my hands to their cheeks, flushed not merely with youth but from the morning's chill. "My dear Lucy," I whispered, smiling, "I would give you half a dozen more."

"Half a dozen more farewells?" she said.

"No, no," I answered, moving nearer. "Children. Sons."

"John James," she said, her eyes regarding me with affection, though she did not put her arms around me but kept hold of the boys. I leaned down to kiss John and then Victor.

"Good fortune is with me," I said, kissing your mother's cheek, putting my hands at her waist. I peered into her eyes and did not wish to turn away. My desire for intimacy with her was always greatest at moments of departure, as though I might carry with me, as I will in the much longer journey that awaits me now, not merely the memory of her but her touch, her scent.

"They are ready," she said, and I turned to see my captain smiling as though in apology at her.

"Must I go alone?" I asked, and your mother pulled the boys close against her, her arms across their shoulders.

"This is not a rough course," I said.

"They are children," she answered.

"They will soon be men."

"Too soon," she told me, and her eyes turned again toward Jacob Aumack. "They are ready, John James. You've delayed them."

I laughed to signal that I had no intention of wresting your brothers from her, but she would not smile. She seemed to have locked her gaze on the young Joseph Mason, who stood at Aumack's side, his rifle resting on his shoulder as though he were a soldier. Hadn't I lured this boy from his parents in just such a manner, your mother's gaze implied, assuring them that I would provide him with a fit passage toward manhood? Hadn't I implied that the boy's skill at drawing would not merely be rewarded by such an apprenticeship but would provide a reliable means of subsistence once that apprenticeship was done?

I well understood, of course, as did your mother, the absurdity of such a promise. In Philadelphia, I had lost two hundred drawings to the gnawing of mice and rats, my only reliable patrons. In Louisville, I had been imprisoned for my debts and had slept on a damp stone floor for a week until a letter arrived from Bachman, my one true friend, who secured my release by means of a promissory note. Once freed, I took your mother and the boys to Henderson, where my black chalk portraits commanded no great respect and were treated as mere diversions concocted by an inconsequential conjurer, one who would offer far greater amusement if he were able to pull a pigeon from a hat or make the coins cradled in his palm disappear. Finally, at the Western Museum in Cincinnati, though I had proved myself an able taxidermist and painted on the museum's walls convincing murals of wooded landscapes and towering mountains and shimmering lakes, I was informed that my services were no longer required.

So we were all hungry and ill clothed. Your mother was

compelled to mend and sew other women's dresses, instruct other women's children while our own risked neglect. But she understood, she said, that I must continue, must set off in pursuit of my birds.

On the shore she finally let go of the boys and kissed me. "Find them all," she said, and I told her that I would.

"You understand that I must go?" I said, pulling away from her and backing toward the boat.

"If I did not," she said, speaking as if to herself, "we would be ill matched."

My heart recoiled from her apparent sadness and from my own, from the memory, always near at hand, of you, sweet Rose, and of you, young Lucy, and of your mother's and my frequent partings and the great expanse of geography and slow passage of seasons by which we must measure our lengthy separations.

I looked at her a final time, pleading for a kinder parting.

"I understand, John James," she said, and she raised her hand as though she wished too to remember me by touch.

But your mother, above all else, is a woman of practicality and reason. She would not understand, I knew, why I would pay three dollars for a watch. Jacob Aumack, the boat's captain, had acquired the instrument in Evansville from the man who made it, who owed him a debt.

On first spying the watch, I was amused by its peculiar construction. The face was handsome but entirely ordinary and conventional. The back, however, was formed not of gold or silver casing but of blown glass of a pink and smoky hue, providing a glimpse of the inner workings, the wheels and catches of the engine. The watchmaker's initials were inscribed on each wheel in script so delicate and fine it seemed spun by a spider. I was struck by the device's cleverness and determined that I must have it. I made my offer, which Aumack, laughing all the while at my undisguised delight, readily accepted.

"When you've acquired your fortune, Mr. Audubon," he said, allowing the watch to dangle from its chain so that I must reach out and grab it away from him like a child, "I'll expect payment equal to its true worth."

"Then you will receive due payment before a year has passed," I replied, an absurd boast that Aumack acknowledged with a wry smile, for surely the captain had been informed of my reputation, the failed mill and trading station I was leaving behind, the debts that remained unpaid, the unpromising fate that awaited me at this journey's end. I could indeed, like a conjurer, make the coins in my palm disappear. I could not complete the deception, however, my daughters. I could not recover the coins from a sleeve or pull them from the air.

Though I dutifully wound the watch each morning, I had little use for it as we proceeded down the Ohio and into the Mississippi, for the precise hour mattered little, the only instruments put to considerable use my rifle, knife, and pen. I shot wood cock and gray squirrels, barn owls and turkey buzzards. I fired at a young autumnal warbler, whose plumage had led Mr. Wilson to identify the bird wrongly as a new species. I shot a fish hawk at the mouth of the Miami River, seven partridges, and a hermit thrush whose likeness I drew, though drawing in the boat made my head ache and my ears throb. I shot a pheasant but failed to take down a single cedar bird though a flock flew directly overhead. I found in the stomach of a Carolina cuckoo two grasshoppers, recently ingested for they remained utterly intact. I spied a brown pelican whose call was like that of the raven and watched the bird settle upon a red maple, its wings as awkward and heavy as a bellows, the maple's branch bending as though it would break.

You cannot imagine, my dear girls, the happiness afforded me by such pursuits. Now and then a blue crane would take flight before us, though not close enough for a shot. I killed a winter hawk and a Mississippi kite and a rusty grackle, the last a beautiful male, which I drew not merely on account of its scarcity but because I admired the stateliness of its gait and the great speed of its flight, swifter than that of the blackbirds darting between the moss-strewn branches of the swamps. I glimpsed a black hawk dashing from the top of a high cypress tree. I listened to the songs of the red-breasted thrushes and felt my spirits revive despite the cold. I observed two eagles in coitus, the female perched on a limb, the male approaching as if swept forward in a torrent, alighting on her, and remaining until he quaked and shrilled and sailed off, the female following precisely the wild arcs of his path, as though, their union accomplished, she would forbid his pursuit of another.

She would forbid his pursuit of another. Do you hear, my girls, how I speak as though of humans and not of mere animals? Well, I suppose I have done so for so long now that I can hardly discern the one from the other.

But to return to my story: although at times I wished for this journey to end — my clothes were reeking and stale, the provisions scant — more often I wished the river endless, carrying me through the seasons and the alterations of plumage, with new broods appearing to replace the old, my eye trained on migrations both northward and south, my notebook's pages filled one day to the next by drawings of feathers and beaks and talons. Some birds I had observed so briefly that I wondered if I had merely imagined them, if I possessed in my mind's eye far more species than those that truly sailed between earth and the heavens.

I consulted my watch only when my thoughts turned to your mother and brothers, as though it might tell me how long I had been absent or how long it would be until I would return. But I soon learned that the watch could tell me nothing, not even the hour, for by the time the boat approached New Orleans — the earthen levee along the river hiding all but the city's rooftops and steeples — it was already useless, its hands swinging erratically back and forth as though it were no watch at all but merely an untrustworthy compass.

Not wanting to place my good and generous captain in the position of returning the three dollars because of my poor judgment, I acted as though the watch continued in fine and reliable operation, pulling it from my pocket to inspect it, glancing down as if to mark the hour, but secretly hoping on each occasion that its life might have been, since last inspection, magically restored.

On my return, I decided, I would make a gift of the watch to John and Victor, or I would offer it for your mother's amusement. *A gift*, I would say, and nothing more, or I would suggest that I had found it underfoot or washed up on a muddy shore. Or I would declare that it had been a fitting reward for some selfless and noble act — fishing a riverman from the swamp in which his pirogue had overturned, or providing a meal to a weary woodsman.

Until then, my sweet daughters, I would determine the hour by the sun. I would mark each day's passage with my paper and pen. I would attend to a single feather, the quietest call, a rustle of leaves.

Toutes gibiers c'est frères moin, I once heard some wizened if
unschooled gentleman remark. *Every bird is my brother.* Yes.
I would find them all.

I must live now, as you see, in the province of women, abiding their busyness, their ceaseless chatter, their tireless devotion. And what man has ever managed to unwind, as they
seem to do, the entanglements of love, its endless careening
toward loss? I have not and will not now — and so can do
nothing but keep to my bed. It is women who must care for
the infirm, the fevered and the dying. Men are of use only to
heft the corpse, build the box, loosen the earth. What use
would I be on my own behalf, my daughters, stripped as I am
of all youthful vitality?

But I have been the luckiest of men. I have you two, who
listen to my aimless anecdotes, my meandering stories. I had
a mother once, twice — and have one yet again, it would
seem: dear Lucy, my wife, your mother, who raises a cup to
my lips, pulls the blanket up beneath my chin, and summons
the girl — who is she? — with the extraordinary voice to
sing to me before I sleep. The children — my granddaugh-
ters, perhaps — cling to the hem of the girl's skirt, hatchlings craning their necks and shrieking.

But you, my daughters, so quiet, so vigilant. I will tell you
again. Your mother is mistaken. They are all mistaken. I am
indeed an old man, and an old man's mind is often addled,
straying from its course as easily as a weary traveler who, in
search of a place to rest, loses sight of the road he has just
left. What man, though, has not found himself in just such a
circumstance, his coat sleeve or trouser leg caught on the
bramble's thorns, his boots muddied, his vision obscured by
swarming insects, yet amid his curses peering into the dis-

tance to spot some tender or captivating scene — a she-wolf languidly suckling her newborn pups, a young woman bathing in a secluded stream, a flock of swallows darting and diving against the setting sun like the notes of a triumphant hymn spiraling magnificently across the page? What man has not set off in pursuit of one thing and happened upon another, more precious than what he first sought — a lost brooch when he wished only for a comb, a woman of exceptional beauty and grace when he had merely looked for her brother or father, the congeniality and comfort of an inn when only a dry patch of ground was expected?

Thus have I found you, my dear ones, after so many years. Thus have you found me.

Before I took to my bed, before this infirmity fully grabbed hold, I took on the jester's role, hiding the hens' eggs about the house and asking the children to hunt them down or allowing the dogs to sniff them out. "Come to me! Come to me!" I would sing, and I would ring the dinner bell at every hour, demand dry shirts from your mother when my dresser was full. I would offer the children chocolates before breakfast and cackle like a ghoul or mew like a cat to amuse them, arching my eyebrows in a feigned scowl that would send them scurrying beneath beds or inside cupboards in ecstatic terror. I would chase them outdoors and watch them climb in the orchard, urging them higher and higher, swearing that I had left a jeweled ring dangling from a branch, assuring the littlest that I would catch them if they fell. And looking up, I would imagine that it was I who climbed these trees, that my youth had been restored, that I could simply stretch out my arms and set off from the highest limb, a rough-legged buzzard become a great white heron.

I wore my age as though it were a familiar, much-loved cloak. I took great delight in your brother John's skilled portrait, in which my hair and beard, though white, seem a lion's mane, the orange and purple glow of the setting sun resting above my shoulder and bathing me in its warm, embracing light.

Now, though, I remember with far greater clarity than the arrangement on my plate of last evening's meal that which I observed little more than weeks after my birth — how the sun penetrated the shade cast by the dense foliage on the Ile-à-Vache in Saint-Domingue, revealing to my eyes, which knew nothing of this world, the spiny rivulets of each leaf, how their colors changed in the ocean's ever-shifting breezes. My mother was no doubt always near at hand to quench my thirst by placing my lips to her sore, blighted breasts so I could drink my fill, my eyes on the faint blue lines beneath her skin as though here were all the branching rivers I might in my life forge or traverse, an embedded map of the earth.

Do you hold such early memories as well, dear sweet Rose, dear young Lucy? Surely you must, for there are no others to which you must attend, no failures of courage or character, nothing but pure innocence and wonder with which to fill your days.

You are without sin, without disgrace, without shame. Your souls unburdened, you can float on the wind's currents, sail through the air.

So they are all mistaken, my precious girls. My noble mind is not in ruins. My wits are not dulled. It is merely that now, confined to my bed, I can do little more than follow my mind's ceaseless meanderings and listen to the sounds that drift through the window. It is not infirmity but the great perspective of age that steers my thoughts inward, toward the menagerie that has taken up residence there in ever-greater numbers, ever-increasing detail, an endless parade of whistles, squawks, and cries, of feathers narrow, broad, and rounded, of bills and beaks and claws and behaviors so closely observed, so well defined, that I find in them a match for every human act: of jealousy, of spite, of devotion, of regret. And of love, always of love, though I have never known how to speak of it, how to explain so consuming a passion. My birds.

They will not be silent. I would not silence them, just as I would not rid myself of your precious company. And they are all here, every one, those I took down with my shot, those captured with a net or a borrowed shawl or my hat, those lifted delicately from their nests, cradled in my palm. Yes, they are all here, though your eyes perhaps do not see them: the plumed partridge and pinnated grouse, the duskey duck and the loggerhead shrike, the night-hawk and wood-wren, the greenshank and great auk, the tell-tale godwit, the tawny thrush, the crested titmouse, the sooty tern. Thorax and stomach, spine and sternum, trachea and liver, tongue and heart — their delicate bodies emblazoned with my knife's red cross, as though I would mark them all, as a rancher brands his herd.

It is not infirmity but passion that steers my mind's course. But how little I possess in these, my final days: a bed and blanket, a window, a cracked bowl and sponge. My thoughts careen from side to side, I know, and spill forth like baggage thrown from a bent-wheeled carriage, their contents dislodged and scattered, covered in dust. But that is not a mind in ruins.

Here is your mother, my dear friend Bachman, your brothers John Woodhouse and Victor. Here are you, my daughters, grown lovelier than I would have dared to hope. And here is the brood of children who dance, perform their pantomimes, cling to the girl's hem.

No, not John Woodhouse: he is hunting gold across the continent, his father's restless spirit blindly guiding him. Not Bachman, not now; he merely writes in indecipherable impatience, which Victor deciphers nevertheless: *Where are the final drawings, John James? The quadrupeds must soon be completed. The printer awaits. All my writing and scolding do no good. I am mad as Thunder, but I trust you are well.*

So your mother and Victor have obeyed my instructions and told Bachman nothing of my recent decline. I wave your brother away but in a brief lucid moment whisper, "Tell Bachman, Victor, that I am almost done."

Who would claim that I do not have my wits about me? My *wit*, at least, for I am indeed almost done. My physician — the man's name? — has confided as much to your mother in my presence, as though I were capable of recognizing nothing, neither their expressions nor their words, not your mother sobbing on his shoulder, not the physician gently, insistently steering her from the room as a lover might seek to comfort his beloved. I observed how he lowered his head, how he too appeared to be weeping. In his hand he held his watch, as though he were prepared to mark the hour of my earthly departure, recording the minute, the very second.

Why would this man weep? Perhaps he is more friend than physician. Perhaps he possesses — despite his trade, despite his witness to a thousand such deaths — a delicate constitution, a pliant heart. Perhaps no man can remain unmoved by the grim spectacle of another man's undoing, for he cannot help but feel that he is acquiring a glimpse of his own.

Thus the physician wept.

The physician weeping, my daughters, a watch gripped in his hand.

The crested titmouse, the sooty tern, the band-tailed dove, the Louisiana heron, the black-throated diver, and the blue-winged teal. The pomerine jaeger, the hooded merganser. Brewer's blackbird. Baird's bunting. The caracara eagle. The blue jay and ivory gull and raven.

I know, dear sweet Rose, dear young Lucy, that you still do not understand, but there is so much to tell you. So many years to unwind and unwind, an endless thread.

So many birds, all here.

Thirty years ago, a wounded sparrow hawk descending in a blind, horrific rage.

Thirty years ago, black crows picking at the charred fields of cane.

Thirty years ago. Could it be so long?

Yes, my mind has wandered far astray, my daughters, but there is reason here. Listen. Thirty years ago, I watched a physician weep — not this same man, of course, but the physician Gautreaux of New Orleans. Observe how I merely shut my eyes and we find ourselves there in Louisiana. The evening has ended; there has been a storm. Through a window I inspect the tattered landscape — the cane fields stripped bare, branches of willow and wisteria coiled like ropes around the trunks of scarred and uprooted oaks, the Negroes' quarters collapsed, their meager contents spilling across the muddy paths: a wooden cup, an iron pot, a leather shoe, a broken stool. Two oxen lie on their sides, chests heaving, their cart overturned.

Where were my birds then? I thought them lost, my dear girls. I threw open the window, but the woods beyond the cane fields had grown silent, utterly still; the birds had been ripped from the sky, were gone forever, slaughtered by the ferocious wind; the world had fallen into an unending, unbearable quiet.

Even now, with my life almost done, I do not feel such terror as I felt then.

And I too remained silent, did not speak, imagining that my every ambition had been rendered absurd and that here was fit punishment for my betrayal of your dear mother, of the sanctity of our marriage. Oh, I must speak of it, I know. But listen to the silence outdoors, the awful silence.

My birds were gone.

The demons Emile Gautreaux and I were to have kept at bay through the long night of our watch had descended not on the corpse of Myra Richardson Gautreaux, stretched on the table before us, but on my own head. I would never manage, I concluded, to unblacken my dark soul, which clung to desire even in the wretched company of a corpse and led me like a lowly, demon-haunted swine to bathe in the foul, dung-splattered mud.

You do not understand, I know.

But see: a moment later, fear left me, for through the window I heard, beyond the woods, the Mississippi rushing wildly, preparing to test the soaked earth, to rise above its banks and race down through the woods and fields as though it had been poured from pitcher to bowl. And above the roar of rushing water I heard an owl calling, as if to mark the dawn, and then I observed a flock of geese heading north, as if in pursuit of the storm. I heard a mourning dove's gurgling, its throaty song.

Even in God's most vengeful and terrifying act, the birds had been spared. All else might be lost, but not the birds.

I turned then, euphoric, my spirits restored. At my shoulder stood Emile Gautreaux. The night was over. Our watch was done. I did not speak, did not tell Gautreaux anything of my indiscretion. I would not look again on Myra Gautreaux's form, would not consider how I might well have had a hand in this poor woman's undoing. I would not carry my memory of this evening forward but would set it aside forever. I would set off in pursuit of my birds.

I have said too much. What father would speak of such matters to his own daughters, would make such a confession before their eyes and ears? But who else would hear and listen and understand? In this bed, no matter how my birds call to me, no matter my resolve, I cannot turn my thoughts from that evening thirty years ago. I might make, like any man awaiting death, a thousand confessions, a thousand acknowledgments of weakness, deception, cowardice, shame, debts unpaid, opportunity squandered. And I would be forgiven. By your mother. By Bachman. By Victor and John. But here is a repentance unaffected, a crime — indeed a crime — unacknowledged. My unforgivable omission.

In New Orleans, unaware of the woman's circumstances, unaware even of her name, I drew her portrait. I drew her as she wished to be drawn and carried her in my arms to her bed and, heedless of my own covenants and obligations, unaware that she was bound by her own, mad with desire —

How could I speak such words, my daughters — not merely to Emile Gautreaux but to myself, to my own heart?

Thus I did not speak. Instead I gave Emile Gautreaux Jacob Aumack's watch. I intimated that it had ceased its operation that very day, perhaps at the very hour when Myra Richardson Gautreaux had died, as though the heavens had marked her passage from this world to the next, had provoked the storm on her behalf, had summoned all the birds and silenced their calls, stilled their wings.

I gave Gautreaux the watch rather than speak to him.

But now, with my own death so near, I must speak. I must be forgiven not merely for my betrayal but for my wretched silence these thirty years.

To whom should I speak, my daughters? I called out to your mother. I attempted to get up from this bed but could not. I called again, and there she was, pushing her white hair away from her forehead. She had been baking bread or cakes and smelled of the flour; her hands were dusted white, her forehead streaked as if with a penitent's ashes.

She was not a penitent, though. She required no confessor.

"I'm here, John James," she said, and there was a contrived lightheartedness to her voice, a wary perusal in her expression.

Would I tell her and undo the knot that has bound us so long? I have traveled throughout this country, from the Florida Keys to the rocky northern shores of Maine. I have journeyed to England and Scotland and Spain, sailed to Labrador and Newfoundland, returned triumphant to my childhood home. Always your mother has welcomed me back with innocent wonder and gratitude, her fidelity unwavering, her faith steadfast and pure.

"A letter," I said to her. "We must send a letter."

And she laughed. "That is all?" she said, and she reached a hand toward my forehead, to see, I knew, if I had a fever, if I was mad with it. I turned my head away.

"You are tired, John James," she said. "You should sleep."

"A letter," I said again, and though I wanted my voice to seem resolute, insistent, it was little more than a whisper.

"To whom, John James?"

Despite her cheerful expression, her pleasant manner, I knew what thoughts possessed her — that soon she would be alone, that my end was at hand, perhaps in a week's time, no more than two, surely before the year is done. Suddenly I wanted nearby, in attendance at my bed, not your mother but the girl — she is Victor's wife, of course, and thus your sister. She is Bachman's daughter. I wanted to hear the girl's voice, as distinct and affecting as the lilac's perfume. Her dress open, my parched lips drinking at her breast, that I might be a child again, an infant . . .

No. I would teach the girl the songs my own mother — my stepmother — once sang to me, when she would have me fall asleep in her arms, though I was too old for such coddling. But it was your mother who leaned over me and touched her hand to my brow.

I heard the rushing water of the Hudson — of the Mississippi. I saw the great expanse of sky through the window. I saw Emile Gautreaux, physician of New Orleans, his shoulders hunched, weeping.

Surely, my precious daughters, the soul must take flight the very instant death grabs hold. Why would it linger? What further business would it have among the living? Thus our watch through the night had been useless. Myra Gautreaux's soul had fled. Her soul had fled from me, for hadn't I provoked her despair, caused her mortal worry that she would be found out, revealed to her husband not merely as an undeserving wife but as an infidel, a temptress, a whore? I had taken her life as surely as one who snaps another's neck or plunges a knife into the heart.

"To whom, John James?" your mother said again, speaking my name as though she feared I would soon forget this as well, just as I have forgotten, from time to time these past months, my successes, the great acclaim my birds have won me, the modest fortune, the precision and grace my hands possessed when they took up both pen and brush.

I lifted those hands to your mother, trembling. I wished to draw her near, confess my indiscretion.

She would not understand. She would think me mad. Or, much worse, she would be overcome by sorrow, devastated by a betrayal unacknowledged these thirty years.

"Quickly," I said, and the rushing water was now accompanied by the wild thrashing of a thousand pairs of wings and a thousand taunting, insistent cries.

"To my desk, dear Lucy," I said. "A letter."

2

Gautreaux's Resurrection

I believed that the world was bereft of miracles. I determined that science, not faith or protestation or prayer, was the only worthy means of inquiry, discovery, or revelation. Then all was lost to me, and I believed in nothing.

And now? Now I would assert that a man's life might be transformed once and then again — and then yet again — not merely by the catastrophic or supremely fortunate events that are impressed upon him but also by the smallest turn in circumstance — a mere word or two, the slightest gesture, a letter delivered by a child.

Whether such transformations are the work of chance or of design, and whether they conform to the laws of the natural world or occur as the result of divine intercession, I am unable to say. All I possess is the knowledge of my own life's story, which, though I remained resolutely silent for so many years, I shall now endeavor to tell.

•   •   •

Slouching in my chair on a winter's afternoon, I was woken by a knock on my front door. The knock was a gentle one, barely audible; nevertheless, it was sufficient to wake me. My eyes opened. My heart raced. My right hand shot out in a wild, palsied spasm, displacing the open volume on my desk: a life of the surgeon Sir Astley Cooper through which I had been idly wandering before I drifted off to sleep. I watched the book fall, the pages fluttering like the feathers of a hawk taken down by a hunter's shot.

With a dull thud, the book struck the rug beneath my feet. Dust rose in the late afternoon's waning sunlight, a blade of that light angling through the study's window and slicing first across my head and then across my chest as I reached for my cane, slowly rose, and called out, "One moment, please!"

Though I could not have slept very long, I had been dreaming nonetheless, the same dream of loss and consolation I had dreamed for nearly thirty years — a dream of my beloved Myra, of whom time had made, in my eyes, a child. I imagined the black ringlets of her hair damp and pressed against her pale forehead and flushed cheeks, her nightclothes twisted to define, as if by an artist's hand, the precise contours of her figure: the swell of her breasts, the arc of her waist and hips, the gently sloping curve of her thighs — a woman's figure after all, not a child's; a woman of such fine and familiar beauty that these thirty years were as nothing at all.

I remembered — though it seemed not memory but sensation — my fingers pressed lightly against her cheek, my hands taking hold of her arms to pull her near, my fingers counting of their own accord her vertebrae, a diagnosis of wonder and surprise, our legs entwined, our arms encircling.

Before Myra, I had thought myself beyond such carnal

adoration, too used to scrutiny, to cool inquiry, to dispassion-
ate calculation. I considered myself an old man, though I was
but forty-two years old and in fine health. I could not have
known I would live so long. But the memories of our encounters, the pleasures of our bed, swelled inside me, as
though even thirty years later I would find Myra waiting,
prepared to feel my weight, my chest pressed against her
breasts, my hips pushing open her thighs, parting her legs
until our bodies were joined.

I did not choose to think of her in such a manner, to recollect our intimacy in such torturous detail. But I possessed no
greater command of my thoughts than I did of my palsied
limb. Both leapt of their own accord, struck out wildly, without restraint.

She had enjoyed my gaze as fully as my touch. The curtain
pulled open, her body bathed in the moon's pale light, she
would invite me to delight in her figure. She would place her
hands upon her breasts, allow them to stray even to the dark
flower of her sex, the *mons veneris*, the *labia majora*. "What
do you wish to see, Emile?" she would say. "What do you
wish to see, my love?"

And I would stammer some pallid reply. "My dear Myra,
my love," I might answer, in faint echo of her words, as awkward and shy as a boy. Once I scribbled a tribute to her that
I meant to say aloud. I longed to compose a song to rival
those of Solomon, to speak of sweet nectar and incense, of
darkness and light and music that would descend from the
heavens to accompany our pleasure. But seeing her, standing
before her, I could not speak. And Myra laughed and announced her own desire; she summoned language so surpris-
ing and bold that I could not help but rush toward her.

She was amused by my silence and gently taunted me, de-

claring that I would study a dead man's body with more freedom than I would her own, though it was she and not the
corpse who had given her consent, who welcomed such attentions. I would conduct my observations of that corpse before an audience of a hundred but would not speak an intimate word to her in private.

What had I known of rapture and passion before Myra?
I had known nothing. I had never encountered a woman
who spoke so freely, who boldly announced her desire and
touched her own body as though her hands belonged to another. I did not understand how she had come to learn a language that would give voice to such forbidding intimacy, a
language that would not merely recount the escalations of
her desire but call out to me, plead with me to speak as well,
to explain precisely how I wished to touch her, how I wanted
to position her for the greatest pleasure from our union, how
she might reveal herself to me and thus stir me toward some
greater summit of desire and freedom and elation.

But in my dream Myra silently rose from her bed, chastely
embraced me, and walked away, her nightclothes twisted
tight around her as though loath to relinquish such intimate
touch. I followed her as she led me through the house and
out to an allée of giant oaks, then into and through a dark
wood, her pace quickening with every step, until finally, with
the advent of evening, she slipped from view. I called out to
her, and though she did not reappear, I continued to trace her
footsteps in the crackle of dried leaves and the snap of broken twigs. From time to time the wind gained strength; the
air was filled with both the sweet perfume of lilac and a
musty odor of decay. For miles and miles, until I awoke, I followed this trail of scent and sound, neither drawing nearer
Myra nor losing the sensation that she was just beyond my
reach.

Another knock, a bit louder, and the dream was gone, replaced by a simple question, the question I had asked and, by my actions, endlessly, fruitlessly answered: *how does a man grieve for thirty years?* And in silence: my ardor unspoken, my passion unsung, as though my voice had been lost when I lost Myra.

"Coming," I muttered, and I shook my head as I moved slowly down the hall, my cane tapping on the floor. The cane's handle was a copper snake, its mouth open, its tongue winding back along the arced body, an absurdly gothic and comical flourish but not one without purpose, for the coiled tongue provided my palsied hand a surer grip. Even so, I raised my left hand near the wall in case I should need further support. My fingers stretched out one by one as though I might be composing in the air a slow and mournful tune.

I would have composed, had I been able, had I possessed the requisite gifts, a dirge, a brooding elegy. Had I possessed the gift of rhyme, I would have written an epic to make millions weep as I had wept. I would have constructed a monument — an impenetrable, unscalable tower — to her memory; I would have painted a portrait of her as she appeared in my dreams. I would have searched the evening sky for a distant star, embarked upon the riskiest expedition to declare her dominion over uncharted land, led the slaughter of millions merely in defense of her name. This was the voice with which I would finally shout out what I had left unspoken in her presence.

This was, I knew, how I grieved.

Just as I reached the door, there was a third knock. "Patience!" I called out, and as I swung the door open, a slight figure, a boy, stepped back into the shadows beyond the doorway.

"Here," I said, and I motioned the boy forward, flourishing my cane like a magician's wand, the snake's mouth gaping as though it were set to strike.

When the boy finally stepped up, I was for a moment appalled. He was dirty and shivering. He was shoeless; his clothes were gray and torn. There were sores at his chin, above an eye, on one arm. He was a beggar, an orphan wandering from door to door in the cold. It was to his benefit, of course, that for this encounter he should wear no shoes, that he shiver, that his face be disfigured with open sores, for pity seeks an adequate impetus, charity a compelling display. But this boy appeared far worse than the circumstance required.

By vague reflex, I considered offering him my attention. I might have announced that I was a physician, searched among my possessions for a balm or lotion to provide him some relief from his sores. Instead, though, I reached with my left hand into my vest pocket and pulled out a few coins. Only then did I see that the boy had stretched out his own hand, that he had come not to beg for alms but to deliver a letter.

"A messenger!" I said, and I brandished my cane and laughed, a hollow exhalation of voice and air. "A noble messenger disguised as a waif!" I laughed again, wanting the boy to understand that he need not be afraid, that this cane, this trembling hand, this gruff demeanor, were little more than a costume prescribed by age, a role I would as willingly have cast off as the boy would his own. But even to my own ears my laughter sounded menacing and grim; thus I stopped and regarded the boy.

"From up north," he said, shivering, his voice deeper, more resonant, than I had imagined it would be. "Postmaster says you wouldn't come and get it yourself." He ducked his head, coughed, then ran a hand beneath his streaming nose. A wet streak stained his hand, and he took another step forward. "Postmaster says if I got more than three cents for this, I might keep what's left for myself."

He handed over the letter, and I gave him the coins. Guessing the postmaster's cruelty, a homonymic trick of the tongue — *What you get is nothing, son, so now you'll have more sense* — I reached back into my pocket. My movements, though, were too slow for the boy, who turned and ran off down the street, weaving around a lamppost, leaping over an empty crate, the pennies squeezed in his fist — a dirty oyster guarding its pearl. I stepped outside and watched until he turned the corner, struck by the peculiar and unsettling intimation that this moment, this exchange, remained incomplete, that I was certain to encounter this boy again or that I had perhaps encountered him before.

After closing the door and placing the letter in my pocket, I made my way back to my study, opened the window, and pushed back the shutters to allow more light into the room — the dull gray light of the winter afternoon. I moved over to my desk, lit a candle, and bent down to retrieve, with considerable effort, the heavy volume from the floor. Before falling asleep, I had been reading how one autumn evening an elephant had collapsed and died at the Tower Menagerie in London, and Sir Astley Cooper had arranged to have the animal transported to his home on St. Mary Axe. The circus performers dragged the elephant down the street, two at each leg, delighted to have found a means of disposing of the wretched and unwieldy corpse so quickly. In his courtyard, Cooper took to the elephant with his knife as the curious shoved one another aside and peered through the iron gate for a glimpse of the bloody enterprise. The slow reduction of the pachyderm to its component parts was observed, the volume's author asserted, neither with bland curiosity nor with abject disgust but with true reverence and awe.

True reverence and awe. The assertion made me laugh.

Half a century ago, while studying in Paris, I traveled to London and made the acquaintance of Astley Cooper. I visited Guy's Hospital, where Cooper held an appointment; I attended his lectures at St. Thomas's. I even visited his home, where, after a dinner of dry lamb and fine spirits, we pored over the shelves lined with great glass specimen jars — knotted hearts, bulging gray brains, a web-footed fetus, curled intestines — and opened the wide drawers that contained a fascinating array of skeletal remains — a twisted femur, a dozen distended skulls, an infant's shattered ribs, the grossly elongated pelvis of adjoined twins.

While most of his colleagues regarded Cooper as more than a little deranged, since his passion for anatomical inquiry was as indiscriminate as it was unquenchable, I concluded that this man's intellect was as sharp and reliable as his knife. Cooper had, I knew, persisted in his studies. He had spat upon his colleagues' mistrust. He had ignored — perhaps even reveled in — the public's recrimination. He had done what I had not.

Cooper's biographer, however, had rewritten the man's life as though he were that life's author. He awarded Cooper laurels where there had in fact been only scorn. With his pen's flourish, he altered history to reflect his own assessment of his subject, unaware that in his effort to champion Cooper's accomplishments, he diminished them instead, as one might polish silver so assiduously that its true character is obscured.

Now I straightened my back, set down the volume, and rested my cane against the desk. I pulled the letter from my pocket and eased into my chair. From up north, I considered, not so much curious as surprised, for without family, friends, or colleagues, I had neither sent nor received correspondence in many years.

But thirty years ago, a strange letter like this one, bearing no inscription beyond my name, was of little moment. My endeavors had gained such wide attention that both my name and my residence were widely known, printed in newspapers and pamphlets, announced with derision from the pulpit, condemned in the public square. Representatives of both church and state declared me a lunatic, an outlaw, the devil's helpmate, a scourge. My figure was hung in effigy and burned at the stake. Legislators threatened laws to prohibit my vile, unnatural inquiries, to match my depravity with an equal measure of scorn. Though I had been generous in my support of the Jesuits and of the sisters of the Sacré Coeur, I was excommunicated from the Church, forbidden to step through the doors of St. Louis Cathedral, prohibited from receiving holy communion or any other of the blessed sacraments. *Emile Gautreaux's purse may be full,* the Very Reverend Bishop McGahan declared, as though his words bore the imprimatur of the papal seal, *but he is in want of a human soul, for his is surely an empty and putrid carcass.*

And the letters — the letters had arrived nearly every day. Myra would put aside her discomfort and sort through them, removing those whose only purpose was to curse my name, declare me an evil, unholy, deluded man, threaten me with some grave harm — the writer's unintended pun, *grave harm,* causing even Myra, despite her fear for my safety, to smile in undisguised pleasure before she committed those words to the fire.

"You are notorious, Emile. You have been branded," she

would say. "Now I can never permit myself to leave your side."

Though she smiled and pretended that such words were spoken in jest, I understood the truth behind them — that my life was indeed placed at risk by my profession, and that her own life might be at risk as well.

The remaining letters, far fewer in number, Myra delivered to me in my study. A handful came from other physicians, declaring their allegiance to my cause and affirming — as if I sought such affirmation — the propriety and scientific value of my pursuits.

I too have traveled abroad and witnessed the fine work of our French and English compatriots, such letters would announce.

I have had opportunity to peruse Laennec's Treatise on Mediate Auscultation *and I am quite convinced of its abiding merit.*

My eyes would dart across the page, eager to find some worthy commentary, some true insight.

Without a complete and decisive knowledge of pathology, our profession . . .

Maligned and misunderstood, we cannot hope . . .

If but one life be spared . . .

It was of no use. "Let them stand at my side," I would say to Myra. "Let them wield the scalpel as they would wield their pens. Let them carry the shovel and sack. Let them fear such retribution and scorn." And I would throw the letters down, asking Myra to commit them to the fire too.

"You would be well advised, Emile, to preserve such endorsements," she would say. "There may be an occasion when you will wish them at hand."

But I would wave at her, and she would obey my instructions and cast the pages into the flames.

The letters I kept, the ones that might indeed prove useful, were the most repulsive. Composed in the common slang of the unprivileged, they were from those who merely wished to secure a few dollars in exchange for handing over a corpse.

Fresh, these letters invariably declared. *A fresh one* — as if death were a ripe fruit, a budding flower, a fattened pig. There were times when my avocation would sicken even me.

It was Myra, always Myra, who by her unwavering endorsement and quiet entreaties prompted me to carry on. "Dear Emile," she might say, and nothing more, with her head pressed against my cheek, her arms thrown about my neck, yet that would be enough to strengthen my resolve. I *would* continue my investigations. I would urge the city's authorities to agree to an arrangement that would provide surgeons with enough cadavers upon which they might practice their craft. How many lives had been lost by a surgeon's incompetence, his unfamiliarity with the very trade by which he would earn his bread? "A radish is not an apple!" I would shout. "Nor is a dog a man! Would you not have the surgeon know what he will encounter as well as you know what you taste on your tongue?"

Unable to persuade the authorities of my logic, I was compelled to heed any missive that might lead me to a corpse. I relied on the services of certain men — a Mr. Caswell, a Mr. Thomas, a Mr. Bunce, a Mr. Sanchez, all as repulsive as those who dispatched these letters — to secure for me suitable specimens for study. I would make my way to a certain dark, stale tavern, order a tepid and watery ale, and hand over the letters to these men as though they were engaged in some grand, intriguing plot — to free the exiled emperor from the island of St. Helena (a scheme concerning which I had once been approached) or to abduct our hapless governor and execute him, if not for his crimes, then for his dullness and cowardice, his far too pliant spine.

Should these men fail, as they often did, to provide enough corpses, I would take to the graveyards myself, lean my weight against the shovel, and proceed to dig. It was a disagreeable business all around, with an eye out for watchmen or late-night mourners or illicit lovers seeking a private retreat, an ear trained to hear the echo of horses' hooves or the dragging footfalls of drunken beggars, who might cry out with maniacal alarm not at the sight before them but at their minds' own imaginings — *A ghost! A ghoul! An evil spirit clothed in a corpse's flesh!*

Once I located a new grave, I had to loosen the earth, find the coffin, apply enough force with an iron bar to splinter the coffin's lid, hook a rope beneath the corpse's arms and around the chest, so that it might be quickly hoisted, bagged, and carried off. Though my aim was worthy, my actions imperative, I could not help but feel at such moments that it was I, not the corpse, who had been defiled, dehumanized, made monstrous and perverse. For weeks after such an excursion I might refuse to read the letters I received, instructing Myra not to sort through them but to set them all aflame.

Nearly thirty years ago, though, upon Myra's death, the letters diminished in number and then stopped, for I canceled my weekly lectures, dismissed my apprentices and pupils, abandoned my study of anatomy. I arranged for the ill-preserved cadavers that awaited dissection to be buried in the paupers' cemetery, for three corpses returned to the very graves from which they had been unearthed two weeks earlier — three corpses around which had swirled such wild speculation, such outrage, such unfounded allegation, that one would think they were the incarnation of the Holy Trinity rather than the remains of three ruffians who'd met a bloody end when their thievery had gone awry.

The bodies interred, my possessions removed from the premises, I sold my surgical theater to a man who gaily asserted that he was planning an enterprise not wholly unlike that which I had undertaken. He too, he explained, would grant admission to those wishing to explore in exquisite detail the body's compelling mysteries.

I feigned ignorance of his meaning. I quickly signed my name to the paper before me and pushed it away as though it were laced with poison.

"These are warm ones, though," the man said, grinning, clasping the document in his hand. "These are alive and all of a piece, if you take my meaning." He leaned near my ear and whispered, his breath as warm and foul as dung, "These are ones you might like to keep close for an evening."

Eager to quit him, I handed the man the theater's keys. "Good luck to you, sir," I said.

The next day I placed a notice in the newspaper that henceforth I would offer my services only as a physician — *in attendance and proper treatment of all manner of physical maladies as are visited upon man, woman, or child, such services administered for reasonable consideration.* I knew, of course, that few, if any, would be willing to entrust themselves to my care — the care of a man known not as healer but as anatomist.

Anatomist. That was my true name, my true calling. When I was disposed to a consideration of such matters, as when I was flush with the warmth of my evening cordial, I liked to imagine myself stepping into the illustration on the opening page of Casserius's anatomical treatise. There, in that fanciful etching, I would stand before the regal goddess Anatomia sitting staunchly on her throne, a looking-glass perched on one knee, a skull on the other. At her sides were Diligentia, smiling coyly, and Ingenium, pointing to her own eyes. A pillar made of a man's skeleton, another of a man's flayed corpse — these provided an architectural flourish to the temple. And I would assume the role of the humble physician come to worship at this altar, kneeling before the table of instruments, looking up in meekness and gratitude, with true reverence and awe.

Anatomist. No man might wear, I believed, a more ennobling badge.

Other terms, though, were applied to me with far greater frequency: *mutilator of corpses, grave robber, body snatcher.* At first I laughed, but as time passed, with annoyance. *Fisherman, thief, stealer of souls.* And my annoyance, as opposition swelled, became rage. *Snatch, grab, resurrectionist.*

Resurrectionist. That appellation, like all the others, was meant as a term of disparagement, suggesting the blasphemy of such men as I — men who would interfere with Providence by exhuming those whose bodies had been assigned until the final judgment to God's holy acre. But I embraced the term nevertheless, for I believed that I was indeed engaged in a resurrection — the resurrection of science in the face of ignorance and suspicion. Would God not smile upon such an endeavor? Would He not view the anatomist's investigation as an act performed solely to proclaim His greater glory, to herald His sublime genius, to declare that if any man should doubt the intricate and brilliant design of the universe, he need only peer inside a human body, observe its organs, its skeleton, its bright channels of blood? *There* was

the proof of a divine intelligence. *There* was the evidence of
an immortal hand. One might devote a thousand lifetimes to
such study and still remain enthralled, bowing one's head in
awe and admiration of the supreme artist who crafted such a
form.

And the practical value of such inquiry was indisputable.
Extirpation required not merely a steady hand but an intimate knowledge of local anatomical relationships. How else
could the physician know that in his efforts to heal, he would
do no harm? Truly, a man is not a dog.

Yet upon Myra's death, I gave up. I left the progress of
science, of medical inquiry and instruction, to other men. I
forsook Anatomia, ignored her entreaties, lowered my eyes
from her gaze. I retired to my study and attempted to engage
myself in quiet contemplation of those mysteries that required no violation of law or faith and culminated in no public approbation. I read philosophy and literature. I attended
concerts, the theater, the opera. When I could not resist, I
read the treatises of fellow physicians and evaluated their assertions, but I did not make my own contributions, did not
resume my own study, did not even, except in the rarest moments, consider it.

I was not a stranger to pleasure, but that pleasure was in
most instances perverse. I attended the lewd displays at the
theater where I had once delivered my lectures. I found the
women, naked or clothed only in the sheerest cloth, stirring
but lifeless, their expressions stark, their skin as waxy as that
of the corpses I had once worked upon. Inebriated, I might
pursue the company of women and lead them to my bed, but
I tore at their clothes in a rage disguised as passion, openly
sneered at their nakedness and my own, coupled as though I
were an untamed beast. And my fury grew greater when I

learned that such jeerings and advances were received not with fear or disgust but with a pronounced and immodest gratitude, as though these women's souls haunted the same dark caverns as my own.

When shame finally steered me away from such encounters, I began an account of my life. *The Resurrectionist*, I wrote across the first page in great sloping letters, and beneath, *The Confessions of Emile Legrand Gautreaux, Anatomist.* But I did not know how to tell such a story — how could I craft an adequate defense, explain in laymen's terms the body's exquisite grandeur? — and I soon placed the few pages I had written in a leather bag, tied the bag closed, and abandoned the enterprise.

Though I forgot where among my possessions the bag containing these pages was stored, I did not forget the final sentence I had written, the words that caused me to stop, which were merely a question: *is it not sufficient that there was one soul, though that soul now be departed, who understood that my life was one not of cruelty but of compassion and that my aim was not to profane but to exalt?*

It must be sufficient, I had decided. It must be enough that one had understood, had shared my passion. She had stood at my side, her thirst for knowledge equal to my own. With my hand — indeed, my entire body — trembling at the recollection of my dearly beloved Myra, I had set down my pen and resolved not to write of her again, or even to speak her name aloud, for words were not, and could not be, equal to her memory. I was not, and could not make myself, a poet.

The dull brain perplexes and retards, the young Keats wistfully declared, and my brain was, despite my years of study, as dull as any, devoid of music or song, a cracked and toneless bell. It was the testimony of a poet that my memory of Myra deserved, a poet who could carve words onto the page like a sculptor carving stone.

> That I might drink, and leave the world unseen,
> And with thee fade away into the forest dim

Such were my sentiments — such was the story that shaped my dreams of Myra — but I could not make the words my own. So I did what I could do. From time to time, until I became too frail, I traveled abroad, where I visited cathedrals and botanical gardens, strolled through ancient ruins, slept and woke and dined in complete and grateful anonymity. On a certain day, at a certain hour, I might suddenly look up at the configuration of clouds, at the rise and fall of hillside and valley, at the dust-strewn patches of shadow in a public square, and understand that I had found a moment of contentment and my life had been briefly but convincingly restored.

But it was precisely at such moments that Myra would appear to me, take a seat at my side, lift her hands to my face. She would lean toward me as though she meant to speak, as though to remind me of the great pleasure we had taken in each other's company — our evenings at the French Opera House, where I would translate the recitatives into awful doggerel; our quiet mornings with coffee on the patio, the plantain's giant leaves forming a bower above our heads; our Sundays wandering among the dancing slaves in Congo Square; our nights of carnality and mirth; our days of anatomical study.

Just as this apparition of Myra would begin to speak, however, she would disappear, along with my sense of contentment, which was quickly replaced by a restlessness of spirit.

Dissatisfaction and rage, melancholy and trepidation, and a grief that recognized no boundaries, allowed no deliverance, and permitted no flight soon engulfed me.

It did not escape my notice that this condition was quite similar to the one that had on countless occasions been visited upon Myra — an impairment that none of my medical training and study had adequately prepared me to address, though I pored through a thousand published volumes. I had watched in confusion and despair what I secretly named, for want of a fitter expression, Myra's *dismantling*. She would become sullen, forlorn. When such spells were of any duration, she would withdraw to the residence I had occupied before our marriage, a modest apartment in the Faubourg Marigny, half a mile from our home, which I had, at her request, refused to sell so she could make of it a private retreat. She would bolt herself inside, allowing only the servant Gabriel to attend to her and deliver her meals, while I endured days and occasionally an entire week of worry and desperation before she finally returned home. I found no ministration, no action, that would reliably repel her dark spirits — precisely as I was unable to find, in the thirty years after her death, that which might repel my own.

Thus I would return in despair from my fruitless wanderings abroad to my home in New Orleans. I returned warily, though, afraid that I might encounter in the newspapers some account of recent anatomical indiscretions — the vanishing of a corpse from the indigents' ward at Hôtel Dieu before the death had been certified, or the discovery of the remnants of a dissected cadaver in Bayou St. John, afloat as though it were a fallen limb. In such instances, the public's attention would be directed to my history, to the vile accusations that time had granted an undeserved patina of truth:

*did not the physician Gautreaux arrange the murder of three men
for the sole purpose of medical dissection and study?*

I did not, but who would hear my answer? I had been in
possession of the bodies. These men's deaths had come vio-
lently, skillfully, unobserved; the knife employed to slice their
throats had been as sharp as a fisherman's, a butcher's, a surgeon's.

Thus was the public's memory altered; thus was a question
transformed into a blind assertion, a simple, indisputable
fact. *Emile Gautreaux was neither scientist nor physician but a
vile murderer.*

It was no use to speak the truth, for even the truth was an
outrage: I had found the corpses, a rare prize, in the paupers'
cemetery, the dirt thrown over them still loose and unsettled.
How was I to know that these men's burial had been performed as secretly as their resurrection was to be? How was I
to know that the coroner possessed no certificate confirming
the occasion and manner of their deaths?

Eventually, though, my notoriety became associated not
with what I had once been or done but with what I had become: a wealthy and childless widower, an eccentric recluse,
a crippled old man to whom was attached some forgotten
history of cruelty and madness. *He killed his wife with an axe,*
children whispered to one another beneath my windows or
outside my door. *He's eaten a man's heart for his dinner, and just
looking into his eyes can send you into a trance. He's got a devil's
tail in his backside, and he's carved the stubs of horns off the top of
his head.* The children repeated these assertions, embellished
them, passed them along as if by repeating them they might
alchemize myth. And they goaded one another toward encounters that none would dare attempt, no matter the prom-

ised reward. If I surprised them by throwing open my door and stepping outside, they cried out in alarm and scurried up and down the street like rats seeking a safe, dark hole.

Again I would set sail for some distant shore, the whispering voices of these children drowned by the crashing of waves, by the staccato shouts in foreign tongues in crooked alleyways and crowded markets, by the narratives I encountered in volumes removed from dusty shelves in dimly lit aisles and then hauled back home to take their place first lying by my chair and then squeezed onto the shelves or teetering on a stack on the floor of my study.

I read late into the night, until my vision had blurred or the lamp had gone out or I had fallen asleep in my chair. I read Vesalius and Vasari, Aristotle and Aquinas. I read Donne's *Devotions;* I read Homer and Dante, Milton and Herbert and Molière. I read the journals of those who had traversed the globe to discover rare species of animals and birds, who had mapped out territories and regions previously untouched by civilization. I read of Christian determination to cause a conversion of Moors and Jews. I read of dark savages clothed only in the juice of berries, of warriors armed with poison-tipped spears. I read with melancholy pleasure the poems of Keats and found there again and again the language of my grief, the very words I could not speak.

> Darkling I listen; and, for many a time
> I have been half in love with easeful Death,
> Call'd him soft names in many a mused rhyme,
> To take into the air my quiet breath

I was not a fool; my despair was not blind. I understood that my grief had become an affliction, fully as damaging, as fatal, as the clumps of tissue I had once removed from the shoulder or throat or spine of a waxen corpse, tissue I would then hold aloft for my pupils' inspection. Their faces would be aflame with amazement, with the frightening recognition of how a body might turn on itself and manufacture its own demise.

I imagined possessing such knowledge and skill that I could extract from my own body, as I had longed to extract from Myra's, whatever despoiled organ prompted such grief. But who can live without heart or liver, without memory or sensation, without hand or tongue or eye or brain?

Now more than ever, I read in Keats's poem, *seems it rich to die.*

Sitting at my desk, wishing for no journey except the one from this world to the next, I slowly opened the letter in my hands. As I began to read, I discovered that despite my painful and crippling frailty, despite my melancholy and the resolute morbidity of my thoughts, one more excursion awaited me. For the first time in years, I would have cause to speak Myra's name.

The letter was from New York, from Mrs. Lucy Audubon, wife of the now famous ornithologist whom I had once so admired that I had resolved to become the man's patron, the man in whose company I passed a single evening when Myra died.

A single evening. Yet how devastating and memorable that evening was. At the Pirries' estate in St. Francisville, to which Myra and I had set off for a holiday, seeking relief not merely from the city's debilitating heat but from the accusations inflamed by my possession of the three thieves' corpses, Mr. Audubon and I found ourselves thrown together in a sacred and wretched task — keeping watch through the night over Myra's body. Yet neither he nor I mentioned what I had concluded by the evening's end — that Myra had not taken her own life, by accident or design. She had not been overtaken by a bout of melancholy or seized by some strange madness. She had not, as I at first believed — as all quietly conjectured — drunk herself to death, no longer able to silence the dark voice that bellowed inside her.

I prayed that come morning, Mr. Audubon would gather everyone around and announce — to general amazement, perhaps to terror and alarm — that for the duration of the previous evening he had turned his powers of observation from the ornithological to the human, and that as a consequence of this endeavor he had learned how Myra met her end. This good woman, I prayed he would assert, was not her own victim but another's. And I imagined that he would slowly, accusingly raise his hand and point out the murderer — Lucretia Pirrie, James Pirrie, their daughter, Eliza, the Negro Percy, the boy Joseph Mason. Hadn't Audubon intimated that Myra bore no responsibility for her death? Hadn't he conveyed in the course of our watch that some attendant mystery was at work, some deception? Hadn't I directed him to see what he could uncover, promised him the very reward he sought — freedom to pursue his ambition?

Yet Mr. Audubon did not raise his hand to point out the murderer. Once the storm was over and dawn broke, he did not speak so much as a word on the matter. And I, by virtue of my profession and on account of the accusations I faced in New Orleans, could not speak myself, could not set about proving the conclusion I had reached. If I were to have opened up Myra's body and performed a dissection, I might have established with absolute certainty what I suspected — that her esophagus and stomach had been choked with poi-

son, that her heart must have raced so wildly against this influence that it could not but stop. But to perform that task
would have confirmed the suspicion that I would take any
life — not merely those of three strangers but even that of
my own wife — in order to pursue my ghastly inquiries and
satisfy my bloody craving. How could I speak, if by speaking
I seemed only to declare my guilt, declare that I was so deprived of human feeling that I would set upon my wife first
with a fatal poison and then with a knife?

If I were to open Myra's body and prove my suspicions
correct, I would merely be requesting that upon my return to
New Orleans, I be placed in shackles, tried and convicted of
her murder, paraded through the public square, and hanged,
not in effigy but in fact. I was too frightened to speak. And I
would as well cast even greater doubt on the anatomist's endeavor. My martyrdom would be useless. It would merely
strengthen the resolve of those who opposed our trade.

So I did not speak. I did not demand that Audubon pronounce whatever conclusion he had reached.

Instead, by my silence I declared myself a coward, and
through the long night of keeping watch over Myra's body, it
was no man but nature herself who rose up, delivering a
storm so fierce that it seemed to give voice to my anguish, to
the great injustice that had been done — an injustice that
would, I believed, forever remain unacknowledged.

When the storm finally reached its conclusion, Mr. Audubon stepped forward and offered me a gift, a watch that he
carried in his pocket, though it had, he said, ceased its operation and would now serve merely as a tribute on this sorrow-
ful occasion. Because he presented the watch in solemn cere-
mony, as though it were a precious token of his esteem, I did
not refuse it, though I wondered why he had decided that

this broken instrument was a fitting gift. I placed the watch in my pocket, thanked him, and forgot it until later that day, when Myra's box was completed and we began the journey back to New Orleans. So great was my despair that when I removed the watch from my pocket, I intended to throw it into our path so the horse's hooves or the carriage's wheels might crush it. Before I released it, however, I peered through the glass and observed that it had somehow resumed operation, that its wheels moved forward and back and caught. Turning the watch over, I saw as well that its face now displayed — though it did not seem possible — the correct hour. I continued to peer at the watch until I was certain that its hands would move, that I had not been deluded. Having confirmed this, I returned it to my pocket, and as a lunatic might do when he believes that the world has acted in accordance with his absurd delusions, I began to laugh.

Now her husband was dying, Lucy Audubon's letter declared, and he had asked to see the physician Emile Gautreaux of New Orleans. So she had written, though she had never before heard her husband speak this name. She had thought at first that here was a fantasy, for her husband had of late taken to inventing encounters. But he had repeated this plea with such conviction that it could not be ignored. He would like to ask, he had said, for this physician's forgiveness — and my hands trembled, not from age, not from my palsy, but from a shudder that seemed to take hold of me in precisely the way I had dreamed of taking hold of Myra, with a grasp so ardent and certain it would resist any contrary force and hold in abeyance the perturbations of spirit by which she was possessed, so that only her tenderness, her lively character, her sweet devotion, would persist.

If these words should mean nothing to me, the letter continued, and if an encounter with her husband stood merely as an unremarkable memory or a phantom of her husband's imagination, I should ignore this entreaty, for Mr. Audubon's mind was often muddled. But he had made her swear that she would dispatch such a letter. If I should feel disposed to answer by paying her husband the visit he requested, I should come quickly, for he grew weaker, his body and mind more fragile, with each passing day.

My forgiveness? Again my hands shook. No one, these past thirty years, had asked for my forgiveness. No one had thought to say that perhaps he was mistaken, perhaps I bore no guilt, should bear no shame — that the deaths of the three thieves and of my wife could not have been caused by me. But for what purpose, by what cause, would John James Audubon wish to make such a plea?

Though I wished to resist any unwarranted conclusion, though I wanted to hold my thoughts in check, I could not: *Audubon did know. Audubon was certain.* Why, then, did he not speak? Why did he not announce why Myra's life was taken, whose hand had struck her down?

God keep him, I whispered. *God keep him a little longer still.* And I set the letter on my desk and touched the fingers of my left hand to the watch in my vest pocket, to Audubon's watch. I ran my fingers across the face as though I might feel the fragile but steady hands beneath the glass and judge by touch the progress of the hour, the passing of every hour these thirty years. With my thumb against the back of the watch, I began to remove it, but instead I let it slip from my grasp. I felt its weight as it settled again into my pocket. Then I reached with my right hand for my cane, encircled the copper handle with my palsied fingers, and struggled — though suddenly it was no struggle at all — to stand.

3

Audubon's Decline

I know, my daughters, that even with the windows thrown open, this room cannot be rid of the awful stench of me, of my withered limbs and papery skin, of my foul breath, of the waste that comes of even my meager diet — though still your mother would bathe me with a sponge, bring in boiled herbs, rub my arms and legs with scented oil. She would as well trim my nails and cut my hair and beard, but I wave her away. My nails have turned brittle and cracked; they are as sharp as a hawk's talons. And my hair falls now about my chest and shoulders. I simply brush it away and imagine it caught in the breeze and carried out the window and then woven, white and impossibly delicate, into the nest of a swallow or wren.

I once observed a Canada flycatcher clutching in its beak a red thread so long that even as the bird perched on a tulip poplar's highest branch, the thread dangled down until it reached the ground. Some months later, I came upon what was surely that very flycatcher's nest, for red veins were running through the twigs and straw, woven among them as though with a loom.

I have seen nests whose construction included horsehair, lamb's wool, dyed feathers, twine, and cloth. I have seen shards of glass glinting against straw and clay and found the bright wings of butterflies pasted to a warbler's hutch. I did not wonder then, though I wonder now, at such accidental beauty. How can these creatures unwittingly create an object that far surpasses any man's most artful design?

Yes, I know. The stench of me, of death. My letter to Gautreaux. I remember, of course, and will attempt to continue, though I would rather speak to you of less weighty matters. Well, the Negro Percy had carefully obeyed Lucretia Pirrie's instructions. James Pirrie's card table, its cherry surface blackened with cigar ash and worn as smooth as soap, was carried to the front hall and set down in the dark corner beneath the stairs. James Pirrie's maps, on which he had documented every stone, twig, and tree of his estate, were returned to their drawers. James Pirrie's books, usually scattered about, were placed neatly on their shelves. Even the portraits of the Pirries, of James and Lucretia and of their daughter, Eliza, my willful and exasperating and alluring pupil, were draped with cloth, as though this family would not suffer even through their likenesses to gaze so long on such a scene: the room lit all around by candles, the windows unlatched but pulled closed, Myra Gautreaux stretched out on the table.

And it was the Negro Percy who gathered up the flowers and placed them in the gentlemen's parlor, leaving them to incline in their vases, their stems like strung bows, their petals like patches of bright cloth. Mignonette, lilies, roses — collected not as a sentimental tribute but as a forthright acknowledgment of the season, of the muggy, mosquito-breeding heat that began in the southern swamps and, as the summer neared its peak, stretched farther and farther north along the river until it made a nasty, putrid business of just about everything — particularly, of course, of death.

I watched Percy at his labor. How strange his features seemed, how strange indeed were the features of the whole dark race, though it was not merely the Negro's physical appearance but some other characteristic as well that caused my eyes to linger on his form. Though Percy had seen his sixtieth year, he remained an impressive figure, spirited but tamed, composed of fine manners and speech but possessing a primitive and wild bearing nonetheless, as though he still felt inside the strength and vigor his body had once possessed and was hard-pressed to refrain from applying himself to some great muscular pursuit.

But it was his eyes that might arouse conjecture regarding this man. His eyes suggested a complexity not typical of his race. Their impenetrable darkness, their prominence, the humorous but striking roundness of the lids — I was reminded of the barred owl, which when observed in the glare of day seems extremely dull, even comic, while at night, when his eyes are following his prey, he is transformed into a creature both mysterious and grand, not so simple after all. In the evening, perched on some high branch, he might follow the motions of any intruder with unwavering concentration, as though he were busy formulating his treacherous intentions, affirmed finally by the piercing tone of his screams — screams so strange and discordant that I had on occasion raised my arms above my head as protection from an apparent confrontation, fully aware that this animal's descent was noiseless, swift, and utterly accurate.

The barred owl is not, in the end, to be feared by man but

merely respected, and I believed the same might be said of the Negro Percy. On fewer than a dozen occasions in my two months at Oakley did we speak, yet we developed a bond of sorts — not friendship, nor even an easy association, but a certain respect, a respect born perhaps of the fact that while I was possessed of my freedom, I was to no small degree as much in the Pirries' command as any Negro, the one by birth, myself by contract.

The encounter upon which my association with Percy was forged occurred shortly after my arrival at the Pirrie estate. I had returned to Oakley at twilight after a full twelve hours' drawing in what quickly became my favorite retreat — the shaded banks of Bayou Sara. There, the magnolias were accompanied by poplar, holly, and beech, all rooted in earth as red as a brilliant sunset. The variety of birds in the trees and overhead were so numerous as to defy all of my attempts to count their number. There could be no greater reminder of paradise, no sweeter solitude, than I was afforded there, and such times as these I imagined that I might indeed not merely undertake but full accomplish my grand ambition: to identify, observe, and draw every species of this country's winged inhabitants, to produce a work of ornithology truer and more complete than any man had yet accomplished. That was the notion which my retreat declared a worthy and attainable goal, and only evening's approach proved sufficient provocation to send me away, convinced yet again that I must maintain silence regarding my ambition, for it seemed then unreachable and absurd.

Returning from Bayou Sara, and in such confusing and contradictory spirits as usually possessed me, I passed along the southern edge of the cane fields and came upon Percy in the company of a small child. Percy was offering instruction on a crude whistle to the child, too young to be his own, though there was an evident tenderness in their encounter. The child's smallest success in producing a musical note prompted in Percy a smile of true delight, and my thoughts turned naturally to my own two sons. I wished that I had the leisure to place my body as freely as my thoughts before such a diversion, a son at each hand or on each knee, the soothing air of a familiar tune providing accompaniment to our pleasure.

Not wishing to disturb Percy and the child's innocent amusement, I said nothing. I meant to continue around the fields and on to the house, but seeing that I was carrying a hawk, which I had taken from the air with a single shot, neither Percy nor the child could tear his eyes from the beast.

I set down my gun and the bag containing my notebook and instruments, and I held the hawk, a swallow-tail, up before them for their delight, spreading the blue-black wings to their full impressive span, showing the creature's snow-white chest, spoiled only by my shot. I then swung the hawk around and provided a fair imitation of its penetrating call, the sound of which had the unfortunate effect of frightening the child. Recognizing a moment later that I was merely acting as a mimic, though, he laughed.

"Would you care to touch it?" I asked. The child, who by my guess was in his fourth year, shook his head and reached for Percy.

So I pulled the hawk back under my arm, retrieved my gun and bag, and turned to go. But to my surprise, Percy begged the animal from me, saying it would make a great treat. I had meant to study it further in my room, fixing it with wire to suggest its sharp angle of descent and the firm grip of its talons on the helpless lizards and small snakes that were its prey. Since such birds were plentiful in this region, I was confident that, come morning, I could easily take down another, so I handed it over.

Percy took the bird as if fearful that, despite the evidence of my shot, it might still be alive. He first brought the bird close to his chest, then held it out as far as his arms would allow, as though he were unsure which risk to undertake, losing the bird or causing himself some harm if the animal should somehow set its wings in motion.

It would make a fine treat, he had declared, but I considered his expression and wondered if I had been the victim of some simple ruse. Perhaps there was a suspicion among the Negroes concerning this creature. There seemed to be precisely such with many others; the commonest pigeon or songbird was revered, while the proud eagle was despised, these suspicions governing the Negroes' behavior to such a degree that the whole dark race seemed utterly foreign and mystifying.

I would have inquired about this matter, for I was interested in the Negroes' customs, particularly in regard to nature and her creatures, but having finally secured the hawk in a manner with which he was satisfied, holding it at its neck with one hand and just above the talons with the other, Percy led the boy away at a rapid pace. Rather than pass around the cane fields, the pair headed directly through them, Percy pausing only long enough to shout, "I thank you kindly, Mr. Audubon." Then they were gone.

After this incident, I observed that I was considered with increased regard by Percy. I learned that the child was Percy's grandson and that three years earlier, when he was not yet a year old, James Pirrie had sold off Percy's daughter Corinne, thus separating mother from child.

When his preparations of the room were complete, Percy peered a moment at Myra Gautreaux's body on the table and then turned to leave the room. I could not help but observe that the Negro seemed shaken, as if he might be overcome. "What is it, Percy?" I asked, and he turned to me.

"Nothing at all, Mr. Audubon," he said, but his eyes seemed blind and searching, and I followed him from the room and out the door. Percy made his way to an oak tree and sat down, his back pressed against the trunk, his hands raised to his eyes.

"Something has troubled you," I remarked, so similar did his reaction to the sight of Myra Gautreaux's body seem to my own.

"That was the beginning of her end," he said, as though speaking not to an audience but merely to his own ears.

"This woman?" I inquired, perplexed by his words. "This business of death?"

Percy lowered his hands from his eyes. "I've got a box to build," he said, and he began to push himself up.

"Wait," I said, placing a hand on his arm.

"Mrs. Pirrie said build the box," he answered, though he did not stand.

"I'll tell Mrs. Pirrie I detained you. What is it?"

Percy peered at me a moment and then settled back against the tree. "I was just put in mind of my daughter, that's all," he said, and he waved his hand in the air as if brushing at a fly. "She wore such a dress of white cotton the day she was led over for her baptism in the river."

"You've not heard from her since she was sold?" I asked.

"She was sixteen, Mr. Audubon," Percy said. "She was sixteen and Mr. Pirrie granted permission so we could use our Sunday rest to celebrate the girl's passage into the savior's flock." The Negro kicked at the ground with the heel of his shoe, a shoe that clearly had once been James Pirrie's. I was struck by the manner in which he spoke, as though his thoughts followed a winding path.

"We wished to wash her soul forever clean," he said, "so we marched down to the river in a great snaking line, every one of us but those nursing strap wounds, for Corinne was a favorite to all, she was so dear and kind." Percy looked toward the house, as if expecting Lucretia Pirrie to step outside.

"Go on, please," I said, aware that he had begun a confidence that caused him no little consternation.

"Mr. Pirrie let us go, sure enough, but he followed the procession down to the river," Percy said, waving his hand in the air to brush away the gnats that had descended on us. "He stood back and watched from a distance as Corinne, smiling all the while, stepped from the muddy shore into the water until she sank down. She held her breath like a child. Her cheeks were swollen with air, and she kept her fingers pinched to her nose." Here Percy imitated his daughter's actions, a scene that would be comic if not for the gravity of his voice.

"Then she pushed herself up out of the water in a giant leap," he continued, "and the water poured off her head and shoulders and chest as if she was truly a vessel of the Lord. She walked back to shore with such quick, strong steps she seemed reborn, not just in spirit but in body as well. And that's the shame of it. That's what he saw."

"James Pirrie?" I said, and Percy nodded.

"That white dress had become just another layer to her skin, and anyone could see how she suddenly looked like a grown woman, just like her mother had before the fever stripped her down to skin and bone. And it wasn't only my eyes on the girl. I knew the whole while he was standing by. I felt his eyes burning like the sun against my back. I just pretended he wasn't there. But he was."

I waited, but Percy was silent. "I've got a box to build," he finally said. "Mrs. Pirrie directed me to build a box. There are better carpenters, but she says build the box, so build the box I will. *By first light,* I told her, and I clicked my tongue like I was considering how rushed I'd be to get the box finished by then. But she doesn't know." Percy looked directly at me, studying my features as I had studied his. "She doesn't know how it should be her husband in that box."

"I could build the box," I said. "You could take on my chore and spend the evening tending to Emile Gautreaux."

"No, sir, Mr. Audubon," Percy said. "I'm more than content to spend the evening down in the low house instead of ten paces from a rotting corpse."

"The flowers," I said. "Did Mrs. Pirrie instruct you to collect those flowers?"

"She did not," Percy said.

"Then I'd like to thank you for them."

Percy nodded. "I'll tell you one thing for certain, Mr. Audubon. There's no flower, not even in the Garden of Evil and Good, that could cover such a smell as that. Just stepping from that room a moment ago I felt I was marking the trail behind me, like I was an unwashed dog who might gain a clear path on account of its awful scent."

"Then I must be one too," I said, and Percy looked at me, nodded, and laughed. I laughed as well, grateful to have had a brief diversion from my task, no matter the grim nature of Percy's tale.

Now I hold my own death in check, hold my breath against my own awful scent, as you girls must do. I await the physician Gautreaux's arrival, not so that he might save me but so that I might save myself.

With no other task at hand, I remember: she was laid out on the table, clothed in a simple white cotton dress, with a gold ribbon in her hair, another at her waist. She seemed to be merely resting there, and indeed, though it had been a full six hours since her death, by some strange magic her skin's hue had not yet begun to change. The room's odor was not that of a corpse but of my own perspiration — and of lilac, I thought, as though this scent emerged from her skin, from her breath.

She is not dead after all, I allowed myself to believe, for the briefest of moments. *I am saved.*

The stench of my body, which will soon make of itself a corpse. This foul and putrid business of death.

My dear sweet Rose, my sweet young Lucy, it cannot end too soon.

4

Audubon's Transgression

You must hear the truth, my daughters. Otherwise, you too will think your father mad. She — my recollection of her — did indeed push me to the edge of reason. I called out to her from the street as though I were a spurned lover. I pounded my fists against her door, begged her to answer, demanded that she answer. Windows were thrown open along the street; men shouted at me, called for order and quiet, commanded me to cease this disturbance. They thought me a drunken vagabond in search of a whore.

I would not cease. Again I pounded my fists against her door. Again I called for her.

But only in St. Francisville, once I had quit New Orleans, did I possess what six months earlier I had sought — her name. Myra Richardson Gautreaux.

With her body before me, I recoiled again from my desire. What sickness of spirit, what ill breeding, would lead me to consider a corpse on a table and take note of its feminine form, would allow my eyes to linger that I might imagine the corpse's life restored, that I might take this woman into my arms again, allow the gold ribbon in her hair to unfurl like bright rings across my fingers, her great surprise at being awakened become something more — her reckless, grateful pleasure?

"Mr. Audubon?"

Do you hear her voice, my daughters, the voice of Lucretia Pirrie, beset by a strange, dry cough? Do you see her ankles as thick as oak roots, her hair as coarse and colorless as straw? I hear that voice even now, I swear. She had stepped beside me; her shoulder touched my own, and her voice was a hoarse whisper, her breath neither sweet nor sour but utterly without scent.

"I trust that in James's absence you will accompany Emile in his watch," she said, and she bent forward and coughed soundlessly.

We looked not at each other but at Gautreaux. He stood near the table where his wife's body lay, murmuring in a low voice that sounded to my ears more animal than human, though he was clearly lost in prayer. A rosary lay curled in his palm, the wooden beads gently tapping against the table's edge as his fingers moved from one prayer to the next. The Lord's Prayer. The Virgin Mary's. Lucretia Pirrie regarded him with an expression no doubt meant to be compassionate but that seemed to me accusatory, a condescending scowl.

If I refused her request, I knew, she would find this sufficient cause for my dismissal, so pronounced and conspicuous had become her mistrust of me, particularly in regard to her daughter. In my first weeks at Oakley, she had found my attention to Eliza and my influence on the girl a cause for celebration. She had marveled at Eliza's sketches, at her

landscapes and portraits, at her studies of the half-tame pea-
cocks, each one of which Eliza named and treated, despite
their apparent disdain and constant squawking, as though it
were a precious child. Eventually, though, Lucretia Pirrie detected my hand in her daughter's works; she saw how I had
disguised Eliza's awkward lines and uneven shading by lur-
ing the viewer's eye to details that displayed true precision
and grace — a flowering tree set on a hill (Joseph Mason's
contribution, in fact), a curiously pensive brow in a portrait
of her father, the bright eye of a peacock's errant feather
peeking out from a boxwood hedge. This, she declared, was a
willful and calculated deception, flattery whose aim was not
to delight but to deceive.

Though at first Lucretia Pirrie had expressed gratitude
that Eliza's attachment to the young physician Ira Smith had
grown less extreme since my arrival, she now claimed that
the tonic which had provided this cure might be of equal if
not surpassing harm. She was reluctant to believe, she said,
that I would calculate such a seduction, but Eliza's infatua-
tion with me was more than apparent, and she had seen me
do little to discourage her daughter's attentions.

"How would I discourage her, Mrs. Pirrie," I protested, "if
the sole purpose of my presence here is to impart to her my
skills?"

But Lucretia Pirrie merely turned away and coughed, as
though she could no longer abide my presence.

Four months earlier, I had chanced to make both mother's
and daughter's acquaintance aboard a steamer to New Orleans. I boarded the boat at Natchez after a series of unsuc-
cessful appointments and had begun to despair of ever providing your mother the money I had promised to dispatch.

When the boat reached St. Francisville, Lucretia and Eliza Pirrie stepped aboard, and I engaged them in conversation. Soon Eliza Pirrie strolled away to watch the gulls that followed in the boat's wake, and I observed from a distance the neat cinch of the girl's waist, the loosened knot of hair at her neck beneath the wind-whipped brim of her hat. I wondered if the girl's mother had ever enjoyed such beauty, and if she now resented her daughter.

If I were to answer that speculation today, I would affirm the truth of my assertion — that indeed Lucretia Pirrie was pained by her daughter's possession of appealing qualities that were no longer her own, and further, that this was what produced her suspicion that I had caught her daughter's affections in my snare.

On the riverboat, however, I merely commented on the girl's delightful manner, and Lucretia Pirrie thanked me and inquired about my portfolio, which I held beneath my arm. With a modest flourish, I handed it over. I was both an artist and an ornithologist, I explained, and I was in search of some worthy enterprise by which I might sustain myself. I found New Orleans dizzyingly gay and yet inhospitable. I would appreciate any association Mrs. Pirrie might recommend.

She quickly studied my portfolio and pronounced my drawings quite remarkable, if somewhat unconventional. Then she laughed.

"Is there wit here as well?" I asked, surprised.

"You depict your subjects not in elegant profile but in startling postures — clutching a bloody carcass, feeding on insects and berries."

"They are drawn from nature," I answered.

"I was merely imagining, Mr. Audubon, how you might execute a portrait. Would you show my husband completing a meal or drinking from a glass? Perhaps he would be shown yawning from remaining still too long?"

"If you wished such a portrait, I might," I replied, and Lucretia Pirrie laughed even more, with some small measure of malice, as though she would take delight in seeing her husband depicted in such a manner. And here too I was correct in my assessment.

By journey's end, though, a happy agreement was forged. At the commencement of summer, I would quit New Orleans, travel to St. Francisville, and take up residence at Oakley to serve as Eliza Pirrie's tutor. In my company would be the boy Joseph Mason, my assistant, who was of very fine character and who would prove, I assured Lucretia Pirrie, no trouble at all. In the mornings I would offer the girl instruction in drawing, dancing, and music. Afternoons and evenings I would be free to keep to myself, to pursue my study and depiction of birds.

I then wrote to your mother: "I have found employment that promises a regular income. The boys will have coats and scarves and mittens come winter. You shall have a new dress. We are saved."

But in time Lucretia Pirrie grew weary of me, even disdainful. Standing beside me in the gentlemen's parlor, awaiting my answer, she coughed again. "Mr. Audubon?"

"Do you not think he would prefer a more private evening?" I replied, glancing at Gautreaux.

"I do not," she said. She glared at me, her eyes daring me to question her judgment, her resolve.

I understood what was being asked of me. Together, the physician and I were to endure the stifling heat of the room, its doors and windows shut as though we would join Myra Gautreaux in her tomb. Here, and through the quiet hours of the night, we were to pray for the safe passage of the woman's soul, to prevent by our simple presence the invasion of her body by such phantoms and ghouls as the imagination might construct in opposition to beauty and goodness and faith. We were to meet the devil at the door if he came knocking, turn him away with an unequivocal display of piety, let it be known to him that the good Lord had left His mark upon this house.

I wished, though in passionate silence, to refuse Lucretia Pirrie's request. I turned away from her and closed my eyes to shut myself off from her, as though I might, by wishing it so, simply erase this woman's gaunt frame from the room. I could imagine no more disturbing circumstance, no greater threat to my hold on reason, than to spend the entire evening in the presence of a corpse — and in the presence of *this* corpse, Myra Richardson Gautreaux, whose name and circumstance I had not previously known, could not have known.

I wanted to shout out that though a young man, I had already had my fill of death, having held not one but two infant daughters in my arms, your rosy cheeks gone pale, your curled fingers turned blue, your eyes' bright light extinguished. And my mother, my true mother, her body wasted save for the full breasts with which she was to nurse me — her death seemed ever-present to my mind, though I had been too young to remember so much as her voice or her touch or the color of her hair.

But I did remember the bloody streets of Nantes when I was a child not ten years old, as the Reign of Terror spread through France, the royalists shot and guillotined, their bodies tied to stones and drowned in the Loire. I had seen my aunt, my father's cruel elder sister, dragged down the street by her hair, bloody heels bouncing behind her like horses' unshod hooves. And I had witnessed, on the Place de Viarme, the execution of the Vendéan leader Charette.

Though my father abruptly removed me to La Gerbetière, our home in Couëron on the banks of the Loire, I returned to Nantes one day, in opposition to my father's instructions, in the company of a servant dispatched on an errand, and there I saw the bodies, hundreds and hundreds of them, awaiting burial. I smelled their stench. I turned away, disgusted and terrified, from their dangling arms and unclosed eyes.

Now I needed to rest, I wanted to tell Lucretia Pirrie. I was feeling somewhat ill, a little faint. My ears throbbed; my head ached. What I needed was sleep, the company my dreams provided me, for it was only through these dreams that I was able to accomplish the journey back to Cincinnati, to lay my hands again on the heads of your two young brothers and then lie down beside your mother and feel her hands travel across my weary body. There, in that dream of approaching sleep, I could listen to the stories your mother constructed for my benefit, a sparrow weaving a nest from the most fragile of twigs, her voice — though it was my dream that provided her words — as tender and reassuring as the touch of her hands on my skin. My skill would soon be recognized, she whispered. My drawings would be adored. We would set sail for England or France, where my renown would multiply and our pockets would grow heavy not with notices of debt or threatening letters but with precious coins.

How long it had been, though, since I had received a letter from your mother, since I had heard of your brothers' progress, received any word regarding your mother's success in finding employment. I wrote to her every third day and addressed my journal to her as well, recording my day's passage, my every errant thought, as though she were looking over my shoulder, eager to remark on my observations. In this journal, in my letters, the words spilled from my pen like rain from a swollen cloud. I would expect her to consider my circumstances, I wrote. I would assume that she understood that I simply desired confirmation of our affection and alliance.

If only a few scribbled words, the briefest of notes, let me always have news of you and the boys, I wrote.

Forgive me, John James, she responded after a month's unbearable silence. *There is always so much to be done.*

"So much to be done," I said stupidly to Lucretia Pirrie, speaking your mother's words out loud, but the woman nodded as though they did indeed signal my assent.

So she left me in that room given over to death, my only company a grieving widower and a corpse — the body of Myra Richardson Gautreaux. Even then I might have spoken her name aloud, as though I were once again standing in the street, banging my fists against her door. I would call out the name that I had learned only upon her death. Why had she not answered? Why had she not shown herself at the window, descended the stairs and summoned me inside, allowed me to explain my actions or silenced me with an embrace, led me by the hand to her bed, revealing herself to me again? Why had she not brought to conclusion what she had begun?

Her body upon the table seemed a fit conclusion, for here was the completion of my shame. Do you understand, my daughters? What had not been completed in New Orleans had been completed with her death. Is it not enough that I make this confession? Must I make one more?

5

Gautreaux's Anatomy

In my youthful travels, I once had occasion to save a life, not by virtue of my knowledge of medicine but by simple chance. Aboard a ship bound for England, for the port at Plymouth, a young woman who had lost a child to a fever a week after the boat set sail had mourned in calm silence throughout the remainder of the passage, peering out at the water for hours on end as though to keep her eyes on the point where her child's body had been lowered into the waves. When we drew near land, however — indeed, when we were but an hour from the shore — the woman descended into what seemed to me a bout of mania. She screamed as though in terror and rushed toward the stern to throw herself into the waves, and I was able to prevent her from accomplishing her aim only because I had stepped outside to enjoy a cigar before collecting my trunk.

The woman struggled to break free of me, and until the ship docked I was forced to hold her in my arms, running my hand through her hair again and again and uttering whatever soothing words seemed to calm her. Once we reached shore, I handed her to her mother, who waited there for her, and explained the circumstance that had prompted this grief. Only then, with her mother's arms wrapped around her, did the woman turn to me and speak. "I failed to tweak his ears," she said, and she smiled at me sadly. "It made him laugh so. I only meant to tweak his ears again."

I was astounded at so peculiar an expression of intimacy. Would she have given up her life to attempt in vain to reach the ocean's depths, and then merely to pinch her son's ears? How absurd was her longing, how debilitated her faculties.

Yes, I was a young man. I understood nothing.

I recalled this incident in my grief over Myra's death. My last affectionate touch, I felt, could not be closing her eyes. It could not be brushing my hand against her lashes, as though she were a child finally overtaken by exhaustion. No, I would keep her always near, I decided. I would pray each day that she might rise like the phoenix or bloom like the heavy bud of the cereus. I would speak to her in whispers, proclaim my love, compose poems and letters that declared in worthy speech every thought I had of her. Had her body been consigned to the waves, I would joyfully swim to the ocean's depths merely to hold her lifeless hand.

What was to be done now, when every reflection would show me her? What was to be done now?

The letter — James Pirrie's letter. Yes, I had handed it over to Lucretia. What else was there to do?

I took Myra in my arms, lifted her shoulders from the table, and embraced her. I knew, of course, that we were not alone — that I was not alone — for I heard Mr. Audubon's breath, knew that he stood at the window. This man would

not intrude again, I prayed, for he had intruded earlier, stepping into the room as I washed down Myra's body and prepared to dress her.

The day's light had vanished. The room was lit by candles,
and the Pirries — Lucretia and Eliza — had gone upstairs
to sleep.

What had transpired here? James Pirrie's plan had been
to return to his estate in our company, but some sudden
complication had compelled him to linger in New Orleans.
Would Myra's fate have been altered if he had accompanied
us? He had said only that a ship in which he held an interest
had been delayed in its return, and he had handed over a letter, asking that it be delivered upon our arrival at Oakley. He
had also insisted that Myra and I make use of his carriage,
for it was loaded with provisions that Lucretia and Eliza
found indispensable — wine and coffee and tea, fine cloths
and curiosities from abroad, items whose delay, he asserted,
they would mourn a great deal more than his own.

James Pirrie had laughed then and cuffed my shoulder, as
though he meant not to hide but to admit freely the truth of
his words — that he held no favor with his wife and daughter, that they would suspect he had lingered in New Orleans
not on account of a ship's delay but in expectation of some
further infidelity. He would join us, he said, upon his return
to Oakley, which he trusted would be soon, and would transport us back to New Orleans once our holiday was done.

As our carriage drew near St. Francisville, we found ourselves a day ahead of our schedule. James Pirrie's horses were
so hearty, so familiar with the roads, that we had traveled as
if aboard a streaking comet. Not wishing to arrive before we
were expected at Oakley, we stopped for an evening at an
inn just south of St. Francisville, where we were welcomed

warmly and afforded a fine dinner and comfortable accommodations. We raised our glasses in salute to the occasion's twofold pleasure: first, we had quit the city and the absurd accusation that I had not merely recovered the three bodies from the paupers' cemetery but ensured that these men had met an untimely and gruesome end, and second, Myra and I would soon find ourselves in the company of John James Audubon, a man who had awakened in me a sense of charity and purpose that I had not known since my youth, a purpose free of the public condemnation that accompanied my own pursuits.

My interest had been spurred by a series of letters from Lucretia that I had received throughout the summer. *We have lately had in residence,* the first of these declared, *a most fascinating gentleman by the name of Audubon, late of New Orleans though a Frenchman by birth, whom Eliza and I chanced to meet en route for our spring visit to the city — a visit when, if you recall, you were far too busy with your profession to entertain us. With a little coaxing — very little, for he readily acknowledged his impoverished state — I succeeded in placing M. Audubon under contract. Though an imperfect and often inattentive tutor to Eliza, he possesses quite a remarkable hand in producing aviary portraits, a pursuit of interest to you, if I recall the diversions of your youth with any accuracy. M. Audubon is himself a most peculiar bird, as stubborn and careless and spectacular as Eliza's prized pets. He wears the woodsman's clothes but exhibits a gentleman's pretension. His hair is unshorn, its ringlets resting on his shoulders as though he were a child whose indulgent, adoring mother cannot bear to groom him. I believe his temperament is, like his heritage, akin to your own, and so you must arrange somehow to meet him.*

This letter, and those that followed, displayed Lucretia's

able hand at joining disparagement and praise, not merely of her subject but of the letters' recipient as well. Such was her means of disguising, on account of her abiding bitterness and regret, a tender heart. Lucretia's disparagement was of little account, but her praise, never dispensed freely, was always deserved.

Thus I had located and purchased a number of works — and these, though remarkable, surely not among his best — that Audubon had seen fit to surrender in New Orleans, and it soon became my intention to pay a visit to Oakley. Though my interest in ornithology had never progressed beyond an exuberant fascination when I glimpsed an unfamiliar bird perched on a branch or balcony, it was an interest that had persisted since childhood. I had delighted in the regal plumage of the bluebird and the indigo bunting, at the dark sheen of the grackle and the crow. I envied these creatures their flight, and envied Mr. Audubon his avocation. It would be both instructive and a pleasure, I concluded, to make the acquaintance of this man.

Indeed, as I acquired examples of his work and my admiration grew, it became my mission to meet him. I must speak with this Mr. Audubon. I must see more of his work, hear of his progress, be apprised of his plans. Perusing the drawings and watercolor studies I had purchased, I became convinced that they possessed some inexplicable and moving power. Might I not have a role to play in Mr. Audubon's grand pursuit, which Lucretia had recounted in her letters? Though a surgeon and scientist, I recognized that I possessed neither the delicate skill of Mr. Audubon's hands nor, of course, his ornithological knowledge. Yet I believed I understood something of his work, something hidden at its very core. I sensed, even in his hurried sketch of a summer tanager and the charcoal outline of a sharp-tailed bunting, the man's imminent achievement, his grand ambition — to show these birds as they had never previously been shown — but something else as well: the disposition that would steer one toward a pursuit whose value few would appreciate or applaud. We were countrymen indeed.

Such a man, I knew, would inspect with full patience and care every feather's curl, every beak or talon's sharp point, the black orb of the smallest eye. There, in the overlay of feathers, in the curve of a neck, in the swell of a breast, in a dark eye, how very much remained to be studied, uncovered, understood. How similar our pursuits, how aligned our professions.

I concluded, as though struck by sublime inspiration, that Myra and I would become Mr. Audubon's patrons. Lucretia's letters had conveyed the man's failures in his efforts to sustain himself and his family, failures that were, Lucretia asserted, as readily acknowledged as theatrically lamented by Mr. Audubon, as though he maintained a certain pride in a devotion that endured even in the face of ruin. And Myra readily agreed to my conclusion. What better use might we make of our own good and substantial fortune, she asserted, which so far exceeded our needs that we had been perplexed as to what might be done with it?

Such was the plan we celebrated at the inn outside St. Francisville. My tongue loosened with drink, I recounted to Myra with a child's delight the precise details. If Mr. Audubon would assent, his family would have a home in New Orleans, a home from which he would be afforded the leisure to conduct his inquiries, produce his exquisite drawings, set off on his expeditions. And he would undertake these endeavors not as he did now, full of worry regarding his family's welfare, but with the serenity of a man who knows that his wife is well sheltered, his children well clothed and well fed.

"We will be the most generous of patrons," I announced to Myra. "We will fill his cupboards with food and our walls with his birds." I raised my glass, touched it to hers. "To John James Audubon!" I said, and Myra met my gaze.

"To Mr. Audubon," she said, and she smiled.

I drank as well to my own prospects. I would watch Mr. Audubon's drawings multiply, as though the birds had been plucked from the air and pasted onto the page. I would witness Mr. Audubon's great oeuvre taking shape, stand at his shoulder to discuss some minute concern — *Does the hemlock warbler truly revolve on the branch in a full circle? Would the wandering rice-bird cower even in the presence of her mate?* Though I did not seek such recognition, perhaps my patronage would be recorded for posterity: Gautreaux's bunting, Gautreaux's nuthatch, Gautreaux's wren. To play the role of Adam with nature's creatures, to give them a name and that name one's own — how closer might one stand to immortality?

And should Audubon possess or acquire an interest in anatomy, he might begin to draw the human body with the care he bestowed on his birds. He might produce a record of his inquiries, illustrations of interest not merely to my apprentices and pupils but to physicians both here and abroad. *Gautreaux's Anatomy, with Illustrations by John James Audubon.*

Such were my thoughts as we celebrated our imminent arrival at Oakley. We raised glass after glass of wine and shared in a bottle of sweet clear rum passed around the inn by a merchant who had just delivered three dozen healthy slaves to a nearby plantation, losing fewer than a dozen others in passage, thus securing himself a healthy profit.

The next day, our celebration continued as we set off for Oakley. Myra extracted from the provisions in the carriage a bottle of the wine James Pirrie had dispatched, and when we were done with that, we stopped the horses to retrieve another and drank directly from the bottle like giddy and reckless rogues. I had never seen Myra so gay, and I suspected that the accusations I faced in New Orleans had proven a greater torment to her than she had acknowledged, and she was thus elated to be free of them for the length of our holiday. When we first set off from New Orleans, she had expressed concern that we might be halted by some authority on behalf of the church and ordered to remain in the city, as though we were criminals whose arrest and execution had been delayed only for the lack of a sturdy gallows.

"We are unfit for polite company," she asserted, though she laughed and drank again from the bottle, the wine spilling from her lips and staining her blouse as the carriage rocked forward.

"We are, I'm afraid," I answered, "unfit for impolite company as well."

"Then we shall set aside all consideration of politeness." Myra brushed her hand at the stain on her blouse as though it were a fly. "We shall merely *be*."

"What we shall merely be, dear Myra, is a scandal," I said.

"We are already a scandal," she replied, and again she laughed. "Have you forgotten?"

"I have," I answered, "and would continue forgetting."

"Though they hunt us down?"

"It is not you, my dear, whom they seek." I handed her the reins so I might drink. "It is not you whose deeds offend both state and church."

"Oh, they do indeed," she said, exchanging the reins for the bottle. She regarded me with a waggish and enticing glance. "They are simply ignorant of my deeds, for mine are far more private. Have you forgotten that as well?"

"Never," I answered. "Never," and I laughed heartily, drunkenly, possessed of wild, childlike joy.

And if I had spoken again as I held Myra's body in my arms, I would have made the very same declaration. I would never forget a moment of our life together, of our union.

Never.

Still holding Myra's body, I turned to see Mr. Audubon at the window. Beyond him, through the glass, I saw a flash of light and heard the roar of a fire. The roar grew louder, the flames throwing their light against the sky, and I imagined that the house, the whole estate, had plummeted into the fiery world of demons, never to rise.

Never.

6

Audubon's Commission

Draw nearer, my precious girls, for I do not wish your mother to hear — not yet, not until I have fully explained all that I do not understand myself. Perhaps your insight is keener than mine. Perhaps you know already the perplexing intoxication of desire, its fearful might.

I readily fixed my eyes on the widower, observing his slumped shoulders and clenched fists, but I could not keep my gaze on the body on the table — not from repulsion or terror but from discomfort at how, no matter the circumstances, I again took account of Myra Gautreaux's features and her feminine form, how I recalled the brief, exquisite pleasure of her company.

A day earlier, when she and her husband arrived at Oakley, I stepped up to the carriage to help her down and was astounded to discover that here was no stranger but one whom I had encountered in New Orleans. I had drawn this woman's portrait. I had drawn her precisely as she had asked to be drawn. But I swear to you, dearest Lucy and Rose, I had not known her name. She had not offered it, and I had not inquired.

So I had not known that she was the physician Gautreaux's wife, or that she was any man's wife — though I knew, of course, that I was husband to another. The house she occupied had seemed to be her own. And I had not known, as I later learned, that she was the daughter of Admiral and Mrs. Richardson, whose acquaintance I had already made, whose home I had entered, whose company I had enjoyed.

She had approached me as I stood outside one of the winter season's quadroon balls. Lacking the dollar required for admission, I was able only to peer through a low window to catch a glimpse of the elegant affair. It was *she* who approached, begging my pardon to ask if I was the artist from the French Academy paying a visit to the city. I wondered later if she knew the truth and meant her words to sting — that while indeed my heritage was French and my profession art, I held no standing in the French Academy and was in fact without patronage of any sort.

"I draw to please myself," I answered, and she turned to gaze through the window at the quadroon maidens dancing in the arms of their companions, the bright plumage of their gowns twirling round and round in shimmering circles.

None of those women, though, were this woman's equal in beauty. Her dark hair framed an exquisite face. What, I wondered, was her place in the evening's society? Was she a participant, a woman of color despite the pale cast of her skin, or merely, like me, a curious observer? Was she a demimondaine hoping to find among those in attendance a gentleman both wealthy and free?

She turned back to me, as though she had been roused from some amusing preoccupation. "And do your drawings please no one else?" she asked.

"I draw from nature," I replied. "Therefore, I must be satisfied with my own pleasure."

She took a step closer. "Would you consider, sir, no diversion from that solitary pursuit?"

"I must consider it," I replied. "Though solitude mends the spirit, it does not mend one's clothes." I held up my arms to reveal the ragged cuffs of my coat, though on every other occasion I endeavored to hide this feature of my dress.

"You would consider, then, a commission?" she said.

I nodded, and she said, "Then I would like a portrait."

Though I was unsure that this was indeed her intent in approaching me — I suspected, I confess, a baser purpose — I quickly consented to draw her likeness. She provided the number and street of a residence, less than a mile from the rooms on Barracks Street that Joseph Mason and I occupied. I asked if the next morning would be too soon for our appointment.

She said that she preferred us to meet that very evening, in a half-hour's time. Before I could object, she presented me with a final glance and smiled vaguely, as though she were humoring me. Then she took hold of her coat's collar, turned around, and headed down the street at a casual pace.

Had I not found the woman's features so pleasing and her manner so coy, I no doubt would have refused to keep such an appointment. Instead I proceeded directly to Barracks Street to retrieve what I needed. There I discovered Joseph reading by candlelight — not his usual study of works that might prove useful in depicting the vegetation to accompany my birds, but a work of poetry by the young Keats, known to me by way of his brother George, with whom I had endured, while residing in Henderson, Kentucky, an unfortunate business fiasco. We had purchased a steam-powered boat that had then been seized by another man, one who unjustly claimed that I had failed to repay a debt. The circumstance remained unsettled, and George Keats's brother, the poet, had dispatched from London two letters on the matter, both of them relying more on insults and threats than on courtesy or reason. Finding Joseph reading this man's work brought the sting of his letters to mind, and I was happy to have an appointment to distract me from any further thoughts as to how to achieve a resolution to that particular entanglement.

Joseph offered a brief commentary on the poetry before him, acknowledging its evocative quality but professing an abiding confusion as to its true aim and purpose, and I paused in my preparations long enough to glance down at the page. The work was a lengthy one that bore the title *Endymion,* and I resolved that I would read a page or two in order to assist my apprentice in his efforts toward improvement. But I found myself too absorbed in keeping my engagement to make full sense of the words, so I merely offered vague encouragement and left Joseph to his own devices, declaring that I would return at some late hour.

The woman's house was one of many narrow structures in the Faubourg Marigny made of copper-tinged brick and wrought iron of the sort favored by the Spanish architects of the city. A Negro answered the door and, without a single word of greeting, directed me upstairs.

There the woman received me. She still wore her hat and gloves, as though she had just returned home, but she quickly removed them. She then raised a hand to her dark hair, looked directly at me, and smiled. I was struck in this lighted room, even more than on the dimly lit street, by her extraordinary features, in particular the pleasing though severe angularity of her face, which provided some ambiguity, a suggestion of a darker mood, to her happy expression, just as a warbler's happy trill may in fact be a solitary and plaintive call to a lost mate.

"Thank you for keeping our appointment, Mr. Audubon," she said, and I started, for I had not at our first meeting offered my name, though I was pleased to have evidence that my skill, if only for likenesses, might have made it a familiar one in this city. I bowed to her and awaited a response, but the woman looked away as though suddenly distracted. When she turned back to me, I extended my hand in greeting. She grasped it and smiled but again did not speak.

Her failure to offer her own name now seemed deliberate, and I found myself reluctant to dispel the air of mystery by inquiring what that name might be. I simply suggested that she find a comfortable seat so that I could begin my work.

She stepped away as though she would sit down but then asked, "Are you able to draw the whole figure?"

When I allowed that I was, and that it was in any case the face and not the figure that posed the greatest challenge to the artist's hand, she replied, "I am referring to the female form, Mr. Audubon. If you do not object and deem yourself capable, I would like you to draw me as though I were an artist's model."

When I failed to respond immediately, the woman smiled again, as though I were an uncomprehending child. "Unclothed, Mr. Audubon," she said, with some measure of impatience. "I would like you to draw me unclothed."

Though I now wish that I had not, I consented, though

with some hesitation — a hesitation prompted not so much by my surprise, which was considerable, as by my fear. My claim to have studied in the studio of the master David might, like my name, be known to this woman. Would she detect that I was in this respect a novice? All art, whether one draws a portrait or a landscape or an allegory, requires a certain detachment of feeling, a concentration of mind and body. But watching her begin to remove her clothing, in a manner both innocent and unrestrained, as though she took no notice of my presence, aroused feelings that left me wholly uncertain of my ability to produce a worthy portrait.

When conducted at a leisurely pace, an elegantly attired woman's disrobing can take no little length of time, so numerous are the latches, hooks, buttons, and bows to be undone. On this occasion I became quite certain that every delay in my subject's progress — a tangled thread, a knotted ribbon — was intended as much to heighten my discomfort and advance my curiosity as to prevent the garment's ruin. I would have averted my eyes if the room had been decorated so as to allow inspection of and comment on its contents, but the walls were nearly bare, the furniture well made but unencumbered by finery of any sort, neither embroidery nor pillows, silver nor vases. The candles in their sconces were the only objects to which I might steer my attention, but these instead merely directed my gaze again to the woman's pale skin, which seemed to drink the light as though it were parched, and to the dark locks of her hair, which fell about her shoulders as she uncoiled the braids in which they had been tied.

Though my aim is to provide you with a complete and detailed record of this encounter, how can I describe for my own daughters that which I witnessed — the woman's figure slowly emerging from the constraints of her clothing, her neck and shoulders and breasts, her waist and thighs, every aspect of her anatomy so rich and intoxicating that I felt I might be overcome? Language is indeed unfit to express the wondrous experience of such beauty, for it makes crude what is sublime. Thus am I struck now, as I was at that moment, by silence, through which I wish to convey to you the emotions that conquered my tongue. I know that I have spoken little here of love — of my fierce and undying attachment to your mother, to your brothers, to you, my daughters, but this love is always present, behind my words. It is contained within my every utterance, though it seems absent, though it might appear to have abandoned me. But I will go on.

Once the woman had finished undressing and stood naked before me, I detected only the slightest suggestion of her embarrassment and discomfort, but the evidence of their presence was enough for me to regain my composure and announce that I would begin my work. She positioned herself on the chaise longue, reclining so as to suggest two contrary sentiments — on the one hand, modesty; on the other, an entire disregard for such constraints. Turned on her side, she allowed one leg to cross the other. She covered one breast with her arm but left the other exposed, and her utter stillness and the flickering lamplight transformed her figure into one of glowing bronze. Now completely still, she became an exquisitely rendered statue, the work of some great master, and I had no reasonable hope of adequately conveying her beauty.

I set about my work nevertheless, and the woman studied me as though she were able to witness the drawing taking shape on the page. Given the confusing array of feelings that swirled inside me, I did not attempt to talk to her, although from time to time she inquired about my progress or expressed an interest in learning my history. Finally I paused to explain that my father had sent me abroad to prevent my conscription into Napoleon's army and to afford me training in the world of commerce. I allowed that while the first of these objectives had been met, the second had not, for I had learned little except how unsuitable a man can be for such matters. The greatest lesson, I explained as I resumed my work, was that I was suited only for the woods and fields, for studying nature's winged creatures, taking them down with my shot, and rendering them on the page.

When the woman expressed surprise that such a pursuit provided full satisfaction, I pretended no offense and merely acknowledged the fear that your mother, left to make her way in Cincinnati with your brothers, might well soon reach the same conclusion.

"I cannot adequately explain my conviction," I said, hoping not to conclude discussion of this matter but to prompt further questions, for no man wants more of an intimate conversation than the opportunity to reveal the engine that drives his mind and heart, that causes him to undertake any risk, to persevere through all manner of adversity and neglect.

And how much more intimate might a conversation be than this? So I began to speak more freely, telling the woman of my travels and my ornithological adventures. But her interest seemed truly captured only when I turned to my childhood. The constant companion of my youth, I explained, was not my sister or any other child but a parrot named Mignonne who liked to perch on my head or shoulder. The parrot was a gift from my father, brought home from Saint-Domingue, and she accompanied me everywhere, even outdoors, and would not fly away, though her wings were often unclipped.

"Such devotion is rare," the woman suggested.

"She loved me, I believe," I answered.

"I was referring to your own devotion," the woman said, and I thought I could detect in her words a veiled reference to some harm, some failure of devotion, that she had herself endured. I would not, then, recount to her how Mignonne had met her end — in the grip of my stepmother's dearest pet, another of my father's prizes brought home from Saint-Domingue: the monkey Claude.

The idea, though, that this woman had suffered some injury had the peculiar effect of rekindling my desire. Might I not sweep away whatever sad reminiscences occupied her thoughts with a tender embrace? Might I not accomplish the same goal on my own behalf with that same gesture?

In an hour's time the drawing was done, and the woman rose and quickly strode toward me, without reaching for her clothes. She regarded the page and then asked, as though she were merely requesting the slightest indulgence, if she could attempt a small adjustment.

I am not possessed of excessive vanity, my dear girls, but I could hardly disguise my surprise that this woman, still unclothed, would presume to alter a work I had at that moment declared complete. It was more than surprise; I took great offense at this circumstance, yet I stepped aside, throwing my arm out and motioning to the page in silent acknowledgment that since she was to pay, she was free to do as she pleased with the work.

How much more satisfactory it might have been if she had been intent only on paying tribute to her own vanity. Instead, though, I watched with no little amazement as she deftly improved my drawing, correcting an errant line, enriching a shadow, suggesting in the features of the face the mystery I had sought to capture but had not.

I was prepared to protest that it was nothing less than a deception for her to refrain from acknowledging her own skill, but without forethought I stepped toward her and, taking hold of her arms with my hands, allowed my lips to press themselves against hers. Gone was my resolve to put aside all desire, to refrain from acknowledging the full power of her allure. I placed my hands on her back and delighted in her kiss, feeling my body respond. I would resist temptation no more.

Here is my shame. I steered her toward a chair and then kneeled before her, my hands and then my lips touching her breasts. Here is how I would draw her, I dared to think — her head thrown back, her legs parted, a display both vulgar and boldly honest, triumphant, complete.

"We must not —" she said, but she stopped, as though pleasure had stolen her voice. I kissed her lips and breasts again, allowed my hands to move blindly down her body until they prompted her to cry out and reach toward my body with her own. I fumbled at my clothes.

"Please," she said, "no." But I would not hear her. I tore off my shirt, touched her again so she would cry out again in pleasure. I would show her attentions that she had never previously known. I would awaken in her whatever flame had been extinguished. I stood, lifted her from the chair, held her in my arms. I carried her about the room until I found the door that opened to her bedroom.

I laid her on the bed. She did not try to turn away from me. She willingly accepted my embraces, the exploration of my hands, and called out her pleasure. Then, as though she had just awoken from a dream, she pushed me away from her.

"I cannot," she said, and she stood up. "We must not —" and she paused as if to stem her passion. "If you would return tomorrow, Mr. Audubon," she said, "you will have full payment for your work." She stood before the door. "Forgive me," she said.

When I stepped past her, she quietly closed the door. I strode about the room like a stalking panther. I returned to the drawing, unable to tear my gaze from it. I had never known such confusion, such shame. Did not this work convey — and not merely convey but shout out like a trumpet's blast — what I had finally acknowledged but had held in check throughout the evening: my every desire, my adoration not simply of the feminine form but of this woman's form, of her nakedness, of her troubling and sublime beauty? My hand had swept across the page as though it were traveling across her body, as though it would touch her breasts, part her legs, attempt to stir in her the desire by which I was possessed.

I would not give up this work, I decided. I could not allow this woman to put on display or even keep in private such an open acknowledgment of my desire. I took hold of the paper, listened at her bedroom door, heard neither sobs nor laughter nor agitation, and raced down the stairs and out of the house.

I was unable to quench my rage, my humiliation, my shame. My dear Lucy, your mother — she had been forgotten. Her plain features, familiar and comforting, had been swept away by this woman's beauty. I could no longer see your mother in my mind's eye. I could not recollect a single feature of her face or form.

I walked to the bank of the river and there clawed at the drawing and tore it in half, tore it again and again. My hands stained black, I then threw the scraps into the river.

It was nearly dawn now, and I walked back to Barracks Street, resolving never again to allow myself to be possessed by feelings like those I had just suffered. I resolved that I would be a true and devoted husband to my dear wife. With Joseph still asleep, I lit a candle, sat at the desk, and composed a letter to your mother as sweet as any I had previously written. I declared my love for her, and my complete devotion. I swore that I would forever remain her worthy, unwavering companion. I then presented an account of my evening, acknowledging the desire that the woman had stirred within me — would have stirred if my heart had belonged to any other but my faithful and devoted wife, my beloved.

When I was done, I decided that I would not send this letter but carry it always in my pocket, near my heart. I imagined, of course, that I might meet the woman again in the weeks before my departure for St. Francisville, as she might seek me out in order to regain possession of my drawing. But she did not.

Though I swore I would give no thought to our encounter, a week later I returned to the woman's residence, knocked repeatedly on the door, and when I received no answer, attempted to peer through the curtained window. I would apologize for my actions — for misinterpreting her return of my embrace, for destroying the portrait. I would explain that I had been displeased with the work, for it had failed to convey her true character, failed to display my skill fully — as she had so readily acknowledged herself in her improvement of the work. I would draw her again, in whatever manner she desired. I must draw her again.

I knocked once more, with no greater success, and then,

though I understood that I might elicit attention, I called out my name, saying that I wished only a moment's conversation. I stepped back and peered up to the second floor, where I was certain that I discerned for an instant a figure at the window, a figure that quickly receded into the dark room.

Again I knocked on the door and shouted. I would speak to her. I would — though this I did not assert — merely look on her again and confirm that I had not imagined that evening when, unclothed, she had stepped toward me, allowed my embrace, thoughtlessly provoked my desire.

Then I felt a hand on my shoulder, and I turned as though a fist had struck my chest and stolen my breath. Three men stood before me, their faces unshaved, their odor sour. The man in the center, the man who had touched my shoulder, tipped his hat at me.

"No better cure for ailing spirits than ale and spirits," he said. He spat at my feet, and the two other men laughed and spat as well. "Perhaps you'd care to accompany us, buy us all a round."

"Please," I said, and though I wished to find a polite refusal, an explanation for a hasty departure, I could think of nothing to say and so ran down the street and around the corner, possessed once more by the shame of my profane desire.

Once I left New Orleans, I swore that I would put aside every thought of this woman. I was grateful that our first meeting had not after all been followed by a second. But my thoughts returned to her time and again and always, it seemed, when I began to draw one of my birds. It was as though my hands wished to produce a likeness not of the creature before me but of her, as though my desire and shame and torment wished to show themselves on the page.

Thus, having seen her again and learned her name, I wondered what Myra Gautreaux's thoughts had been regarding the prospect of seeing me at Oakley. Had she planned to speak to me in private to gain my assurance that I would not mention our encounter or the portrait I had drawn? Had she feared that I would disregard her circumstances and present a full account of the evening, perhaps even producing the drawing for her husband's appalled inspection? And my mind could not resist moving to a final speculation — had she drunk so much, drunk herself into an everlasting sleep, because of her fear that she would be exposed? Did I bear some responsibility for her death? Did I bear all responsibility?

But I had not known her name, and it was *she* who had approached, *she* who had asked for such a portrait, *she* who had welcomed my embrace, *she* who had called out in pleasure at my touch. I had done nothing except respond as any man would respond.

Thus I could not look long upon her body, for even in death she retained her beauty, the same delicate, pale features as her mother. Should I have recognized those features? Should I have asked her name? She was alone in the house where I visited her. There was nothing to suggest a husband, nothing that conveyed her family bonds.

I had made the Richardsons' acquaintance shortly after my arrival in New Orleans. With spirits nearly as bereft as my purse, I was relieved to no small degree by their agreement, once they had seen my portfolio, that I should draw Mrs. Richardson's likeness. The admiral was so pleased by my success that he offered fifty dollars for the work, twice what I had been prepared to ask.

"Have you given any thought to publishing these?" he inquired when he looked at my marsh hawk, hermit thrush, and brown pelican, accomplished along with eight others during my first week in the city. I had sent the others directly to Lucy for safekeeping and to remind young Victor and John Woodhouse of their father and the cause of his prolonged absence.

"I have not considered publication," I declared, gripped as ever by simple modesty. I expected the admiral to insist on their worth and suggest that perhaps among his circle of acquaintances he could find any number of subscriptions for such a work, but the gentleman merely repeated his appreciation of my fine hand.

Perhaps it was not modesty but humiliation that prevented me from admitting my true ambition. There I stood, nearly penniless, my coat and trousers clean but badly worn, my hair unshorn and tangled, offering my services as a portraitist to any gentleman or lady in want of a few hours' amusement. How could I sit in a drawing room or parlor in expectation of receiving some paltry sum and acknowledge that this was not at all how I wished to exercise my talents? How could I explain, while reproducing a face of plain and unremarkable features, my conviction that nature contained a thousand species more interesting, more vibrant and alive, more challenging to the artist's hand and eye than any human?

So to the admiral, and to all others who might ask, I relied on silence to preserve my dignity, my subtle disguise: John James Audubon, portraitist extraordinaire, no loftier in talent or ambition. And worse, perhaps: a debtor, a fool, a raconteur whose stories did not fail to bore, a hobbyist, an amateur, master to an apprentice whose skill far exceeded his own, an unworthy husband, no father at all to his sons.

No. That was not the truth. The truth was something else,

something more. Why, though, should I feel compelled always to speak of my grand ambition? Why must I announce my great plan to strangers? *I will make Wilson's* Ornithology *seem like child's play. I will locate and draw every one of this country's winged inhabitants. I will produce a work of such magnificent beauty, such precision and grace, that every man of learning will recognize and honor my name.*

I would not speak such words, would not welcome derision and doubt, would not hold myself up to ridicule. I would keep my silence and pretend to aspire to be nothing more than I seemed — a mere painter of portraits.

At times, though, I felt the lie was so apparent that my subjects were studying my features as fully as I was studying theirs, that not just this one lie but my every deception might be exposed. I felt sure that my drawing would be interrupted by a sudden exclamation: *Are you not Jean Rabine of Les Cayes, Saint-Domingue? Or is it now Jean-Jacques Fougère of Nantes, bastard of great pretension, son of a whore dispatched to her rightful punishment, brother to a dark-skinned brood?*

Was that how the truth would finally come to light, with some acquaintance of my father's stitching together an account of my true history, a history neither your mother nor your brothers have heard? My mother was not, as I would have people believe, a fair Creole of Louisiana whom my father took as his wife, but a poor French chambermaid, a girl little more than Eliza Pirrie's age, who made her way to Saint-Domingue on the same vessel that carried my father from his wife and home in France to his island estate, a sugar plantation much like the Pirries' plantation at Oakley. Even before the ship landed at Les Cayes, the liaison must have been accomplished. Each evening the sickening swell of the ocean must have been made tolerable for these two pas-

sengers by thoughts of their next encounter, my father let-
ting himself into the girl's quarters, stripping off his clothes,
reaching for her, guided by her quiet, forbidden call.

Had I ever known such passion? To reach so fevered a
pitch, must an intimate act be as my father's was — unsanc-
tioned, illicit, profane? My nearest approach to such desire
was my evening with Myra Gautreaux, an evening that resulted not in conquest but in shame, flight, and torment.

Now, in the Pirries' home, I could not keep my eyes from
her. I was certain that at any moment Gautreaux would turn
to me, see how my eyes followed her body, and raise his voice
in an anguished and chilling cry. *No sin, no matter how secret,
will go unpunished!* I imagined him shouting, his clenched
fist raised, the rosary a talisman to mark the authority with
which he spoke.

On how many women had I allowed my eyes to linger?
How many had prompted such desire that I felt helpless,
overcome? I did not marry your mother for beauty, for sen-
sual pleasure; I married for companionship, for kindness, for
a tender heart.

I chose well, my daughters. Please know that I am certain
I chose well.

Thus I again ask myself that torturous question: what
sickness of spirit, what ill breeding, would cause my eyes to
linger on a corpse?

And my answer: no matter my shame, no matter my attachment to your mother, if Myra Richardson had woken, if
she had not rushed herself to this fate, I would have taken
her into my arms again. I would have torn the gold ribbon
from her hair.

And today? How would I choose today?

I am too old, dear girls, to contemplate such a question.

Instead I hear Gautreaux's voice, which comes to me as though in a thunder crack. *No sin, no matter how secret, will go unpunished.*

Emile Gautreaux did not turn, did not speak, and my thoughts moved again to my mother, young Jeanne Rabine, stepping onto the shore of Saint-Domingue, already carrying my father's first and only son, myself. In my mind's eye, even the girl's landing in what must have seemed to her an exotic paradise is ominous, though my mother was of course unaware that before her first week was done she would meet another of my father's mistresses, a mulatto known to all by her pet name, Sanitte, a woman who had already borne to my father four daughters and would bear one more.

It was to this dark woman that I, only six months old, was handed over once my mother had taken her final breath. How fully she might have recoiled if she had known that within his first year, her darling son would stare up at features he was too young to know were not those of his true mother.

Yet I did know. Or I came to know. I was but three years old when my father, frightened by the dark clouds of rebellion that had begun swirling over his beloved island, left Sanitte, abandoned his plantation, and set free his slaves, never to look again on Jeanne Rabine's grave. On his return to France, he took only two of his children — his son, myself, renamed Jean-Jacques Fougère to disguise my true parentage, and the infant child of the mulatto Sanitte, the only one of her daughters whose skin was light enough to allow her entry into France without suspicion — my dear sister, Rose Bonitte.

I do not know what became of the other children or of Sanitte. My father did not speak of it, and refused to answer my innocent questions. But I learned of the island's history. I knew of the children's, of Sanitte's, likely fate. My father once said — no doubt without thought of his mistress — that not even the corpses on the island were spared; they were dug up for whatever scant treasures might be unearthed: a gold ring hooked around the bone of a finger, a sword strapped to a fleshless hip, a watch like the one Gautreaux removed from his vest pocket and turned distractedly in his hands without looking down to consult the time.

The time. How many minutes, how few, had we passed in this room? How many more remained?

I considered the watch I carried in my own pocket, a worthless fancy.

That I continued to keep that watch seemed, in such a stifling and dreary circumstance, a further reminder of my uncertain character, my unwillingness to allow truth its rightful place in my every word and deed. Perhaps here was sufficient explanation for the fact that since my arrival in this vast country eighteen years earlier, I had set myself to wandering, waking each morning to feel the earth rise and swell beneath my feet, unconvinced that there was indeed, though far below, a solid core.

Come morning, I decided, I would put all pretense aside. Perhaps that would be the use of this sleepless night; that would be the gift I received in return for my gift of accompanying Gautreaux in his watch.

Come morning, this grim penance done, my every sin would be forgiven. Henceforth I would speak only the truth, hiding neither my history nor my ambition. I would compose and hand over to Gautreaux a letter intended for his wife's father, a letter expressing my great sympathy and regret over his daughter's death, then telling the admiral that his question about publication had stirred my interest and asking what his thoughts were on the idea.

How improper it would be, though, to make such an inquiry knowing full well that the man had just lost his daughter, who had ended her life in blind drunkenness, reckless debauchery, enslavement to vice. *In fear of revelation? In mortal fear?*

Peace to her soul, I whispered, as much of a prayer as I could manage and spoken, I must acknowledge, for my own sake as well as the woman's. I looked at Gautreaux, who was still standing beside his wife's corpse, turning his watch in his hand. Is this how we would pass the time, in silent and endless contemplation, as still as Myra Gautreaux on the table?

I turned away from Emile Gautreaux as though I too, like the shrouded Pirries, could not bear this sight. Striding over to a window, I thought for a moment that the whole of Oakley had been set ablaze, that some great inferno had swept through the woods and the cane fields and would soon overtake the house. But no, it was James Pirrie's Negroes, one hundred men or more, and a handful of sturdy Negresses, all preparing to cut the cane at that late hour by the light of a dozen fires.

I should go to Gautreaux now, I told myself. I should make a show of my sympathy, summon some portion of my own sorrows, acknowledge my role in this sad turn.

But I remained at the window to observe the strange tableau outdoors, which by some frightful magic or limitation of the eye seemed not two hundred yards in the distance but painted directly on the glass. Each of the dark figures seemed sketched in careful, sinuous detail, each of the dozen fires shaped by an expert hand, created of a thousand different hues, a swirling of color and light that in an instant, and again and again, expired into a thick cloud of smoke darker than the Negroes themselves, darker and more threatening than a storm pitching through an evening sky.

A storm, I remembered. *James Pirrie's letter. There will indeed be a storm.*

Behind me I heard a noise, an exhalation. I took a step back from the window but did not turn around, for I could see, reflected in the glass, Gautreaux embracing his wife's corpse. His head rested against her breasts. His hands, placed beneath her shoulders, lifted her, and her head fell back, her mouth open as if in a silent, ghastly cry — just as she had thrown back her head when I placed her in the chair, when I dared to touch her.

Then Gautreaux was still, and I saw that this image, this reflection of an awful embrace, was cast in the window directly at the center of the Negroes' fire, as if the physician Gautreaux and the corpse of his wife had both been carefully, intentionally set among the flames.

Peace to our souls, my dear sweet daughters.

Peace to my own soul, for it remains tattered and dark and in ruins.

7

Gautreaux's Preparations

I was unused to being out, so frail had my limbs become, so reclusive my life. On Royal Street, though, I was obliged to set down my case and stand in the cold outside the Banque de Louisiane, the sky growing darker as evening approached. With greater and greater force I rapped my cane against the door. Finally an upstairs window opened, and after a polite though unequivocal entreaty to the young and ill-mannered gentleman inside, who at first insisted that I would have to wait until morning to conduct my business, I succeeded in gaining entrance and securing the considerable sum I required.

I succeeded only because when I announced my name, I spoke as though I possessed the authority to insure that, should I be required to wait until morning, this young man would promptly find himself without employment. It may have been that I did possess such authority, for my father's fortune played no small role in this bank's establishment. My father's dusty portrait still hung inside, his precisely combed gray hair and stern expression suggesting that he would, even in death, make careful note of each transaction. The name Gautreaux was etched on a gold plate affixed to the frame — a name that, when shouted from the street, produced in this young man a tremor of recognition and fear.

After quitting the bank, I walked down two doors to the apothecary Peychaud, who made his residence upstairs in rooms that bore the distinctly medicinal odor of the items dispensed on the floor below. I knocked on the door, waited, then knocked again. Peychaud appeared in the doorway and attempted to hide his surprise at encountering me there, my cane raised before him in a grand and obviously mocking salute.

"Would you refuse business on account of the hour, Monsieur Peychaud?" I inquired. "That seems to be the current philosophy."

"Not at all, not at all, good doctor," Peychaud replied. "I was merely surprised." And with bent back and arthritic gait, he led me inside and along the dusty shelves, reaching up with hands that shook even more than my own to secure the items I requested. I had resolved that if Audubon's affliction was one that might respond to my attentions — though I was quite certain that would not be the case — I would arrive with the means to administer that care.

Peychaud kept up a steady patter of exclamations as we proceeded down the aisles. "Monsieur Gautreaux! Monsieur Gautreaux!" he shouted. "A surprise and an honor, sir!"

His voice was nervous and shrill, as though standing before him now was not the man whom thirty years earlier he had despised and betrayed by providing a variety of exaggerated and plainly false accounts regarding our transactions, but that man's vengeful ghost. Though Peychaud claimed that I had asked him to join me in the resurrection trade, it was in fact he who had asked me, asserting that because his occupation kept him apprised of the activities of each of the city's physicians and because he was well informed as to the identity and condition of their patients, he could alert me to those who possessed a malady that might, when their souls had departed, prove to be of particular anatomical interest.

"I know half a dozen already who might be worth your attention," he declared one evening during intermission at the opera.

"Indeed," I said, peering here and there, hoping to find Myra amid the throng.

"There's a giant, an Irishman seven feet and more, who's taken ill," Peychaud said, leaning toward me. "He's gone to the charity hospital, I hear, where they've pushed three beds together so he can stretch his legs. You might like to see the whole of him, I am sure."

"My interests reside not in what is unusual but in what is common," I sharply replied. "The uncommon astounds but does not instruct, though I suspect you might find certain men willing to meet your price. There is always a market for the freakish."

Peychaud recoiled. "I was merely aiming, understand, to serve your needs. I wasn't giving a single thought to my own."

"Of course," I replied, and I strolled away.

While the subject of the Irishman was never revived, from time to time Peychaud would summon me with news of exotic ailments and their alleged cures or accounts of foreign seamen who had a day earlier stepped ashore at the city's port only to meet a quick and violent end, stabbed or shot or choked in a drunken tavern brawl. Peychaud suggested that he might, for a coin or two of consideration, learn where these men's bodies were to be interred.

When I offered the man silence and scorn rather than the payment he sought, he declared, "I am aware, sir, of the anatomist's requirements. I am well informed regarding the resurrection trade."

While I understood that these words were designed to frighten me, I knew as well that the man was base and possessed of great avarice, and that one penny's payment would only lead to more.

He was also a coward. Though he might speak to the city's authorities regarding my endeavors on behalf of my anatomical inquiries, he would not consent to make those accusations public, for he feared above all else the swift arrow of retribution. A man deprived of both good judgment and morality cannot imagine that others might possess that which he does not.

While I have asserted that a man might be transformed, there are those who prove themselves immune, and I was quite certain that, despite the passage of so many years, here before me stood such a man.

"I'd hoped you were well, Monsieur Gautreaux!" Peychaud lugubriously exclaimed. "I'd had no news of you but hoped, of course, you were well!" He turned to me and, as he handed over another bottle, raised an eyebrow as if to signal his question. "I trust these are not for you, sir? I trust you have not become your own patient?"

"I have not," I replied, and I said nothing more except to thank him when I pulled the coins from my coat pocket and placed them in his trembling hands.

"May you remain in good health, sir," Peychaud said as I

departed, and I could not compel myself to respond in like manner.

Back outdoors, though it was now fully dark and the lamps had not yet been lit, I proceeded down to St. Louis Street and called at the home of Felix Grima, who once conducted a carriage service but who for two years, his son informed me, had grown steadily more infirm of mind. The son turned his head and stepped to the side to signal that his father was inside and that I might look in on him if I liked, but I explained that I must secure a carriage immediately.

"Are you heading north, sir?" the man asked, and I said that I was. "Then you'd do well to take a steamer up the river," he said. "It will take you as far as Louisville."

But I explained that I would prefer a carriage, for I had made far too many trips at sea. I did not explain that passage upon the water, even the calmest river cruise, stirred in me a strange foreboding, an acute sense that I was and had been for many years wandering with aimless purpose, attempting to dispel my grim spirits.

I was advised to inquire on Dauphine at the home of a Spaniard named de Sedella.

Again I set off. I found the Spaniard's residence, promptly made my request, and again removed the leather bag of coins from my coat pocket. De Sedella was unable to contain his enthusiasm when I agreed to his exorbitant fee for a Negro and carriage to transport me to my destination.

"He should call at my home by nine tomorrow morning, no later," I said. "My bags will be ready."

"Very fine, sir. Very fine," de Sedella chimed, my payment clenched in his fists just as the boy at my door that afternoon had clenched the few pennies I had handed over.

"Once my business is completed, I expect to return

promptly," I said. "All told, it should be less than eight weeks, though it may be longer."

"Of course, of course," the Spaniard said, bowing to me, his smile revealing two crooked rows of gray teeth. "You will find Antoine, I assure you, a capable and trustworthy guide. The finest of Negroes, sir."

I stepped away from the door even as the man continued to speak, suggesting that if there was anything else, anything else at all I should require, Antoine would be sure to provide it.

Returning to Royal Street, I proceeded at a slow pace. Ahead of me, the lamplighters were at their work, their torches blazing as they moved from one lamp to the next, as though I had summoned them to show me the way home.

Twice during my walk I believed I had spied up ahead the dirty and shivering boy who had knocked on my door that afternoon. I tried to hurry, my cane tapping against the ground, my feet shuffling so awkwardly I nearly tripped — but then the boy, or whoever it was, turned a corner and disappeared.

I was dismayed that I would again be gripped by absurd superstition, but I could not help but acknowledge the sensation that the boy was a wraith beckoning me toward some shadowy realm or a confrontation of considerable consequence or danger. Perhaps, having peered inside my home and observed my possessions, he believed he might craft a means to effect a theft.

No, he was merely a child. I shook my head to cast out such ridiculous thoughts. I slowed my steps again and proceeded home.

My arrangements complete, I once again sat at my desk before Lucy Audubon's letter, the oil lamp pulled close so I might again decipher its contents. Beneath the letter, opened to its depiction of the yellow-billed cuckoo, was a folio from Mr. Audubon's *Birds*. In the illustration, the female spreads her feathers and cries as she perches on a branch and looks down upon her mate, who holds in his curved, pointed beak a monarch butterfly. How was it that Mr. Audubon depicted the male turned away not simply from the observer but from his mate, as though he would feast alone on this treat, ignoring his mate's entreaties? My own study of birds, though incomplete and unscientific, had suggested among this species a greater harmony, a more generous inclination.

Through the years and by various means I had acquired a substantial collection of Mr. Audubon's illustrations, though I had never taken my own subscription, preferring other methods of acquisition — hunting them down among the meager offerings of the Royal Street book dealers or stumbling upon them, dusty and unexamined, at the home of some wealthy but wholly uncultured merchant, the sort of man my father was.

This was the manner in which, thirty years ago, Myra and I first acquired examples of the young Audubon's work. I had preserved as well the letters from Lucretia that offered her extravagant if unschooled assessment of that work. Initially I kept the letters in case there should be an inquiry as to why Myra and I had left New Orleans for a holiday at Oakley. *As you see,* I imagined myself saying as I handed over the letters to some dimwitted constable or clerk, *we left not because of these preposterous claims but simply by invitation, for the opportunity to make the acquaintance of so remarkable a man. I am extremely fond of birds, as all men must be, for how could we not envy their grace, their capacity for flight, their ingenuity?*

But I would not leave it at that. If they thought me a lunatic, a lunatic I would be. *I think I might like to be a bird,* I would announce, *though I cannot decide between the horned owl and the kingfisher, the wren and the jay* — and on and on until I had grown so tiresome, so apparently deranged, I would be dismissed straight away.

Now I hunted among the papers in my drawers until I found these letters, tied with a frayed string, their pages brittle and yellow. *We have lately had in residence* . . .

I came to know Lucretia in childhood. We were neighbors in the Faubourg Marigny and, in those years of innocence, the dearest of friends. For a time it appeared that we might marry, as our temperaments were well suited. We had learned from our fathers — both of whom were émigrés and cotton merchants and dealers in slaves — a general swagger, a quick dry wit, a sharp tongue. Our mothers had been friends and had died within six months of each other, which increased our attachment, as though our affection for each other diminished the sting of so terrible a misfortune.

Near the time when I began my apprenticeship in medicine, Lucretia's father purchased the estate at Oakley. He was one of the first men to test the notion that sugar cane could be grown to full ripeness in Louisiana, beyond the tropical islands' eternal summer. Thus Lucretia and I were removed from each other's company. It should have been, of course, no insurmountable divide, but it seemed so. We traded letters. I promised to see her when the opportunity arose.

But the opportunity did not arise, so enthralled was I with my studies, and Lucretia was allowed to visit New Orleans only in her father's company, when he had business to conduct. A year later, her father took ill and died, and I thought she might return to the city. But she did not, whether out of allegiance to her father's ambition or out of necessity, I was not certain. Despite her father's efforts, the cane had not thrived, and perhaps she was seeking a buyer for the estate. Or perhaps she had sworn some vow to her father that she would not abandon this place but would see his aims fulfilled.

Whatever the reason, she wrote to tell me that she would not return, and thus the choice I faced was made clear. I could remain in New Orleans to pursue my profession, or I could move to Oakley, marry Lucretia, and reinvent myself as a planter.

I did not go. Such was the great sway of my own ambition, far more powerful even than the heart's affections. I did love Lucretia, as one might love a sister and perhaps even more, but that was not enough. I would not put my profession aside, and as she could not tie herself to my fate, I would not tie myself to hers.

When my decision was made, Lucretia acted quickly. Within a year she and James Pirrie were married. The next year she bore their first child, her daughter Eliza. There would be four more, though none of the others survived through infancy. The last one, her only son, was stillborn. She had written to ask that I be in attendance at the delivery, for she feared that the child, having grown quiet within her, would not be well. I had consented and taken a carriage to Oakley. It was I who took hold of her shoulders and embraced her so that she would not have to look on her dead child. She grieved for months, and, I believed, ever afterward.

Our friendship continued through the years, and I even grew somewhat fond of James Pirrie, despite the man's many failings — fonder, I sometimes suspected, than Lucretia herself was. After Myra's death, however, our correspondence ceased. Only from a newspaper account did I learn a dozen years later of the Pirries' deaths in a fire that spread from the cane fields to the house. I was reminded, of course, of the burning cane on the evening of Myra's death, my evening in Audubon's company, though such thoughts still possessed so sharp an edge that I would not dwell on them.

At my desk, with Lucy Audubon's letter before me, I felt such grief again. Looking down at the letter, at the feminine hand that had written my name at the top of the page, I realized for the first time that the letter bore no date. It might have been dispatched weeks and weeks earlier, and this trip, for which I was so ill prepared, might well be in vain.

I decided to speak the man's name, to call out to him — *John James Audubon!* — and listen for an answer. I wished to know whether he was still alive, if he still lay on his bed or had already met his end, so that his body was enclosed in its coffin and the coffin sealed, nailed shut, buried forever beneath the earth.

Forever? But a corpse cannot ask for forgiveness, cannot beg for mercy, cannot speak. Hadn't Myra, though, spoken my name as I leaned over her and held her body in my embrace? Hadn't she saved inside her a final breath so that she might allow my name to form on her lips?

No, I answered. *No.*

But my heart's answer?

Yes.

8

Audubon's Gaze

Yes, my dear girls, it was the prospect of a storm that had aroused the Negroes, for James Pirrie, in New Orleans to complete his summer business affairs, had sent word of the storm's approach by way of Emile Gautreaux, the most unfortunate of messengers.

Though I was moved by Gautreaux's grief and wished to offer him some small measure of comfort, I did not turn from the window. I felt my ears throbbing again, a condition that had come and gone for some months and about which I had hoped to consult the physician. Each time the throbbing began, I felt as though I were aboard a boat passing across the wake of another, the world bobbing up and down before my eyes so rapidly, with such quick and alarming force, that my sense of balance was threatened and I had to reach for a wall or a table or, as on this occurrence, a windowsill to keep myself upright.

When the throbbing diminished, I opened my eyes to see

three crows descending into the cane fields. Lured by the light and smoke of the Negroes' fires, they descended heavily, devoid of grace. Black as pitch, omnivorous, they would feast with full and equal delight on fruit or vegetable, snake or frog, worm or grub. Given the opportunity, they might even gnaw at the coarse edges of the snapped cane, stripping the stalks thread by glittering thread as though they were gathering golden straw for their nests. The Negroes swung their knives, however, and sent the crows back into the dark woods, to some high branch where they might resume their cackling conversation and summon the courage for another vain assault.

I turned. Gautreaux had now let go of his wife. Though he stood in silence beside her, the light from the candles flickered against his frame and created the illusion of movement. Then he did move, his shoulders rocking, his hands stretching out to clasp his wife's hands, one atop the other at her ribboned waist. He was weeping.

I could not turn away again. "Perhaps, sir —" I said, and he lifted his head to regard me. I motioned to the door, signaling that if he wished me to leave him alone in his grief, I would do so.

He released his grip on his wife's hands. "No, no," he said. "Please. It was I who asked Lucretia to inquire —" He waved a hand at me. "Please stay."

"Yes," I replied. "Of course." I returned my attention to the Negroes' activities. I could hear, even through the closed window, the knives slicing through the cane, the shouts and laughter, the spit and roar of the fires.

Gautreaux crossed the room to stand at my side. He made no comment on the blazing fires but instead said, "Will there truly be a storm?" He peered through the glass and frowned. "There was no sign of it when we left New Orleans. James said nothing, though perhaps he did not want to signal his alarm."

I detected on Gautreaux the scent I had noticed earlier, when I took Myra Gautreaux's hand and helped her descend from the carriage — a sweet scent, unidentifiable, lavender perhaps. Looking at his reflection in the glass, I felt relief at the man's calm expression. Perhaps the madness of new grief had passed.

Only hours earlier, though, when his wife had collapsed, I had wondered if he were wholly stripped of his reason. Kneeling over her, he had looked up at me, his eyes red and swollen. "It was joy," he cried. "It was *joy* that prompted such intoxication." He stood and brushed at his coat. "How, sir," he said, "can joy contain a deadly sword?"

I attempted to think of something I might say in response, but I could think of nothing beyond my own encounter in New Orleans and the conclusion that I had somehow played a hand in Myra Gautreaux's undoing.

Gautreaux leaned toward me then as though he would offer a confidence. "I would like to know," he whispered, "how *joy* might steal a woman's very breath. How" — and then he was shouting, arms swinging in the air so that they would have cuffed me if I had not quickly stepped back — "how can *joy* strike such a cruel and damaging blow?"

"She was struck?" I asked, puzzled and frightened.

"Struck!" Gautreaux cried out in anguish. "She was struck!" His eyes darted about wildly, as though he were searching for some object or person, as though he now saw a world of ghouls and demons swirling about him. "She was struck!" he cried again. "Who would strike —"

Then he collapsed next to his wife, and Lucretia Pirrie rushed forward, put one hand on his back, and with the other motioned me toward him. "Upstairs, Mr. Audubon," she whispered while her hand traced a circle across Gautreaux's back. "Take him upstairs."

I am unsure why, except for my despair and confusion over Myra Gautreaux's death, but instead of fulfilling this request, I began to step away from Gautreaux and his wife as though I had been confronted, my actions in regard to this woman exposed.

"Upstairs!" Lucretia Pirrie said again, shouting.

Thus I moved forward and placed one arm beneath Gautreaux's neck, the other beneath his knees — but before I began to lift his body, my eyes turned to Myra Gautreaux. I peered into her lifeless eyes. What dark passion had swelled in her breast that she would drink herself into this everlasting sleep? How could one so young, possessed of such beauty, meet such an end and with such deliberation? She had drunk so much so quickly, and in private, as though she meant to prompt her swift ruin. Then she had emerged, stumbling, incoherent. She had laughed and then gasped, as though she were drowning. She had fallen neither forward nor back. She had merely lowered herself to the floor as though she would faint.

Had she looked at me? Had her eyes met mine?

Gautreaux seemed as old as my own father had been when he died. How had this woman come to marry a man twice her age? Surely there were men whose youth and vigor might have better matched her own, men who would devote themselves to her pleasure, whose attentions would excite in her an inextinguishable flame, who would have caused her to cling to life rather than abandon it.

Might not I have excited such fervor? Might not I have saved her rather than prompted her ruin?

But these thoughts so disgusted and terrified me that I felt certain Myra Gautreaux was somehow marking my presence, and marking the appalling desire by which I was suddenly possessed. I looked down at Gautreaux, whose breathing calmed though his eyes remained closed. I thought then of how I had held you, dear sweet Rose, and you, dear young Lucy — how I had held your lifeless bodies, bundled as though the blankets held nothing at all, and lowered you into the ground, your mother at my side, weeping and inconsolable.

What worth is this sad confession to you, my dear daughters, whom I was given no opportunity to nurture? But you must know how you have grown in my thoughts. Can it be that you are no longer my dear sweet girls? Were you to show your angelic faces, were you to step out of the shadows, would your youth have quit you, as mine so long ago quit me?

Have I spoken only to the air, to a dim memory? Have I made my confession only to this room's silence? Would you even know your father, dear Lucy, dear Rose? For I no longer bear the faintest resemblance to the man who wept at your birth, who wept in anguish when I held each of you to my breast after your sweet souls departed for heaven.

Do you see how I am weeping still and will weep until I draw my final breath — and beyond, should I not join you in heaven?

That is why I speak — that I might join you.

It was you who held my every thought as I kneeled, secured my grip on Emile Gautreaux, and prepared to bear his weight.

It was not until some hours later, once all confusion had subsided and Myra Gautreaux's body had been placed in the gentlemen's parlor, that James Pirrie's letter was discovered. Emile Gautreaux, composed now, sat in the next room, encircled by those who had stayed near to offer whatever comfort and assistance he might request. Lucretia and Eliza Pirrie sat beside him on the divan, Joseph and I in two chairs drawn near, the Negro Percy just beyond the room's open door.

Gautreaux told us, in a hushed and weary voice, of their time at the inn, their happy anticipation of a holiday at Oakley. Then he reached into the breast pocket of his coat and looked up with dismay and embarrassment, as if he had just recalled some urgent, unattended task.

"Lucretia, forgive me," he said, handing over the letter. "James gave me this as we left. I forgot. I'm very sorry."

"I'm sure it is nothing of consequence, Emile," she said, but she quickly excused herself and retired from the room, as if she expected the contents to be of a personal, perhaps unsettling nature. That might well be the case, I thought, for prior to James Pirrie's departure for New Orleans, I had witnessed any number of unpleasant exchanges between husband and wife. In fact, their accusations and recriminations were so animated that I would locate Eliza and steer her outdoors with charcoal and paper for an impromptu lesson in drawing from nature, borne by the hope that such a tranquil endeavor might diminish her agitation of spirits at hearing her parents quarrel.

I soon learned that Eliza, despite her youth, was adept at both prompting and escalating such quarrels, securing the confidence of her father by posing as a sympathetic audience and then disclosing, in an apparently artless manner, these confidences to her mother. She would in turn report her mother's angry retorts to her father — so that while the girl seemed a helpless ingénue, she in fact possessed both her father's wily recklessness and her mother's vengeful pride, a concoction as inflammatory as powder and flint.

On this occasion, however, whatever alarm the letter might have produced in Lucretia Pirrie turned out to be unwarranted — at least in regard to the private disputes of husband and wife — for within a few minutes she descended the stairs and placed the letter in my hands, announcing that it was addressed not to her but to Mr. O'Connor. "Would you be so kind, Mr. Audubon," she asked, "as to see that he promptly receives it?"

Eager to leave Emile Gautreaux but feeling that it was my duty to remain, I was prepared to suggest that my apprentice would be a worthy messenger. I even turned to Joseph and began to hand the letter over, but Lucretia Pirrie quickly reached for my arm and silently conveyed, with a slight lowering of her head and a glance, her desire that I deliver the letter myself.

Her intention must be, I surmised, that I learn the letter's contents, so once I had passed beyond view of the house, I unfolded the pages and looked down. After asserting that his delay in returning to Oakley was unavoidable, James Pirrie explained that he had, while conducting his maritime transactions, secured reliable information that a powerful hurricane was presently sweeping up through the Gulf of Mexico and was certain not only to damage and perhaps destroy a number of ships in which he held an interest but to strike New Orleans with all unholy force. The storm's likely course, the letter suggested, would be northward, along the curving line of the Mississippi — in which case Oakley would lie precariously near, if not fully in, its path.

I was unable to turn from this first page to the second, because at the door of the low house I was met by the overseer, a coarse but generally affable Irishman, who shut the door behind him as though he were determined to prevent entrance.

"Mr. Audubon," he said, planting his feet in the doorway. "Are the women in need of no further comfort?"

Rather than answer or even attempt to discern the true intent of his question, I handed over the letter.

O'Connor read through its contents and then shook his head and cursed, a gesture I correctly interpreted as disdain for any effort, and this one in particular, to lay claim to a foreknowledge of nature's course. The storm might turn or stall, he declared, shaking the letter in front of my eyes, his thick fingers leaving a dusty imprint on James Pirrie's pages, the ink smudging as though it were not yet dry. The storm might exhaust itself in its progress inland, he continued, or even reverse its course. He trained his eyes on me as though he expected a contradiction. If he must — and he kicked at the dirt, managing to soil my boots — he would wager his life a thousand times over on a storm failing to touch a particular spot of earth.

I attributed the man's exaggerated response simply to his general character until he handed back the letter with the second page placed on top of the first. There, James Pirrie allowed no uncertainty or contrary speculation: to avoid the misfortune of absolute ruin, the cane was to be cut down, cut now, four months prematurely. Cut that very evening.

"Too young," the Irishman declared when I looked up from the letter. "Though it boil for a week, the cane won't strike, I say. We'll lose it all on account of such caution."

With these words he stepped away from the low house and looked up to study the sky, which was blue and cloudless, as if he might find there a signal to confirm or deny the accuracy of James Pirrie's conjecture.

"Mr. O'Connor," I began, hoping to offer him the benefit of my opinion, which was that the remaining hours of daylight might best be spent observing the behavior of certain species — the wild goose or gannet or lestris, even the great brown pelican if one could be found sunning itself on the banks of Bayou Sara. Any of these birds might convey — by the patterns of their flight, their chosen perch, or the manner of their feeding — some signal of the storm's approach, for they were all much finer prognosticators of the weather than their human counterparts.

Before I could offer such advice, however, O'Connor again shook his head. Then he marched off toward the Negroes' houses — little larger and of worse construction than the box in which Myra Gautreaux was now to make her home. There soon came a clamor unlike any I had previously heard, a chorus of cries and pitiful wailing louder than the ugliest choir of demons, and above it all, O'Connor's shouts and curses.

Thus did I observe, outside the window, the Negroes at their labor. James Pirrie's letter remained in my pocket as though I and not the overseer bore responsibility for insuring that the cane was cut. The large, heavy knives the Negroes employed in their labor were not unlike those of a butcher; the cane snapped like the quick split of bone. I watched the knives flash and shine in the fires' flickering light in a rapid rise and fall, as on a moonlit night aboard a skiff one might see a school of silver fish leaping out of the dark water again and again, only to disappear, their motion so quick and astonishing as to place a question before all judgment — was that fish or not? Only the moonlight? A mirror image in the water of the sky's million stars?

But the swing of the knives was certain, for the heads of the cane fell in a flash of light and then the cane itself in the next, the black hands working to strip the stalks of all foliage and tie them in tall faggots. Then, with a great heave and shout, their bearers threw the faggots directly onto the ox carts, four beasts to each cart, yoked to form a considerable if reluctant alliance. With the force of a whip to their hindquarters, they stirred in unison from their natural lethargy and set off for the low house, a brief but treacherous journey, since over the years the oxen's hooves had carved a muddy track down the slope, the full weight of the cart pushing against them as they descended. In the course of the evening and through the night and on until the chore was completed, the cane would be delivered to the low house, where it would be bruised, pressed, boiled, and made into sugar.

These miserable wretches, I thought — meaning, I suppose, both Negro and ox. But that evening I would happily have assumed the place of either rather than attend to the business thrust upon me — conducting that grim vigil, keeping watch through the night with this poor gentleman whose wife, by her own ill judgment or by the summoning of secret demons, had become so intoxicated that she had fallen into an everlasting sleep.

Peace to her soul, I whispered again, and Gautreaux, standing by my side, raised his right hand to lay it on my shoulder. But his hand fell to his side as though he could not bear the exertion of even so small a gesture. Outdoors, a full cart set off from the fields and disappeared down the hill, appearing as if it had been swallowed in a sea of mud.

Would the Negroes manage to cut so much cane before

the storm arrived, if it arrived at all? On a few occasions I had stepped inside the low house, observed its pitched roof, its wide chimneys, its great open windows. I had seen the trenches where the fires were lit, the great iron pots where the cane was boiled. I had admired the industry of it, the miracle of so sparkling and sweet a substance emerging from the hellish flames and the blackened residue of crushed and scalded cane.

Now, turning away from Gautreaux, I cursed my ill fortune. I was as unfit for the present chore as I had been for any of the unsuitable enterprises I had been compelled to take up in my thirty-six years, the myriad business engagements, transactions, and negotiations from which I had always emerged penniless and distracted, requiring the solitude and splendor of nature to restore my spirits.

It had been eighteen years — half a lifetime — since my father had dispatched me from France to this strange, vast country. I had entertained the Pirries and all others who would listen not merely with finely crafted descriptions of the creatures I had encountered in my wanderings but with a full account of my ill-fated adventures — how I had moved, with your mother and brothers in tow, from Pennsylvania to Kentucky and then on to Ohio in pursuit of one trade or another, how I had finally left my family behind, in all great sorrow, to follow the migrations of my beloved birds and render them with a precision and care that no man had previously shown. I had been a miller and merchant and speculator, a taxidermist and teacher and painter of portraits — all against my true inclination, all with no uncertain measure of revulsion and regret.

What is more, I had left behind a trail of debts, with little prospect of repayment. For all I knew, there were men in each of the states I had made my home — and as near as New Orleans, which I had so recently left — who would swear that if their paths ever again crossed my own, such debts would be repaid in blood.

I had found at Oakley, though, what I had so long sought. Who would forsake his claim to a place that offered so much — such solitude and splendor, so very many birds? But confined now to a single room, if only for a night, I felt as I had as a boy of eleven, when my father, tired of my inattention to my studies, put me out to sea. I set off for six months aboard the *Instituteur,* six months of *mal de mer* and of longing for home and the gallery of curiosities I had collected there: the birds' nests holding their delicate unhatched eggs, the lichens and flowers gathered from my stepmother's splendid gardens, the feathers and pebbles retrieved from the banks of the Loire. How many hours I had spent ordering and inspecting my gallery, guarding it as though it were a fortune in gold — hours and hours, days and months and years, that seemed now to have passed in an instant.

But this evening, the evening of my wretched watch — this evening the time passed very slowly indeed, so much so that it appeared to stand still, like a hawk poised over its prey. I turned back to Gautreaux, who, though he still gazed out at the dark sky or perhaps at the Negroes at their labor, no longer wore an expression of grief. He seemed wholly composed, his mouth relaxed as though at any moment he would smile, clap his hand to my back, and announce that our watch was done, our vigil complete. I wondered if perhaps his thoughts had turned to some sweet recollection of his wife. Could such great sorrow have found in memory a ready antidote, a speedy cure? Or perhaps here was only a fleeting moment of relief.

Yes, the relief was illusory — for behind us, though I

would not look, lay the man's young wife, her skin aglow but only from the candlelight, this woman whose body I had touched and would have touched again, whose allure could overwhelm all reason, whose cries of pleasure were a song I would hear still — that I do hear, my daughters, though I am loath to confess the persistence of such vain and inglorious passion.

If I could have managed a true prayer, it would not have been a modest one. I would not have asked simply that this woman's soul be guided to heaven; I would have asked that her eyes be opened, that she rise up from the table as if from a restful sleep, that she step toward us, her face illuminated not from the candlelight but from the ecstasy of a life restored. No lesser prayer, no humble and resigned entreaty, was worth uttering, and for a moment I imagined that prayer answered, imagined her stepping forward — not toward her husband, though. Toward me, her arms reaching out.

Before the watch commenced, my girls, Lucretia Pirrie had offered to wash the body down and dress it, but Gautreaux had refused, insisting that he would perform the chore himself. Though the doors were closed, the curtains drawn, I had stepped into the room quite inadvertently as Gautreaux went about this solemn task, and one might have assumed the man had been caught in an intimate act, the way he turned his head sharply and leaned forward to cover his wife's naked body. His expression was one of both anger and surprise, though once he heard my hurried explanation for the accident — that I was searching in vain for my notebook of drawings, darting from room to room with ever greater urgency and distraction — his eyes conveyed his forgiveness, and he resumed his chore even before I had stepped out and shut the door.

Looking behind me, I saw the man run a cloth over his

wife's face and neck as though he were a mother attending to an infant's bath. I saw the cloth sweep across her breasts, cover and uncover their pink buds — just as my hand had swept across the page to draw them, just as my hands had reached for the dark pleasure of her sex.

The moment the door was fully closed, I heard Gautreaux's voice. *Does he speak to me?* I wondered, and I pressed my ear against the door. No, it was to his wife, who could no longer hear any human voice. Though I understood the violation, I lingered a moment longer, considering how strange was a man's speech when cast like a stone into a still pool of dark and unwelcome silence.

Does my speech sound thus, my dear sweet Rose, my dear Lucy? There have been times when I have found myself alone in a thick wood at evening and have spoken merely to confirm my presence, to assert that indeed I can still speak, have not become just another lumbering presence huffing and snorting, looking here and there.

Perhaps, then, I considered, Gautreaux's words were not so strange. Peering straight into the handiwork of death, indeed having cause to touch it, the man had found himself in a region lonelier and more desolate than any wood, and he had merely made fit expression of his sorrow, of his conviction that there had not been enough time to say to his beloved wife all he wished to say, all he *must* say or else the rest of his days would pass in regret.

Now my ears throb, my daughters, as they throbbed then. The room seems to spin.

No, it is not some ghost, not Myra Gautreaux whom I desire. It is your dear mother. It is she whom, if I had the strength, I would pull near, embrace. It is she, if I were suddenly restored to health, whom I would lead to the bed, de-

lighting in how she unburdened herself of her clothes, stepping out of them as though she were a sea-maiden rising
from the foaming waves. It is her voice I wish to hear, her
pleasure I wish to discern in her raised hips, her bright call,
her rapture and my own. I imagine now, absurdly, though I
have imagined it before, that we might take to the air, our
dalliance like that of the eagle or hawk, our arms become
wings, our skin downy feathers, our pleasure announced in
sharp, melodic cries.

The throbbing in my ears quieted, my daughters. The
room no longer spun. *Dear Lucy. Dear wife,* I thought then
and think now. But my eyes turned as if of their own accord.
My eyes would not be kept from Myra Gautreaux's form,
from memory, from the dark and wretched corridors of
desire.

9

Gautreaux's Suspicion

Yes, though I remained silent so long, I would speak now to all who would listen — to Myra, to John James Audubon, to every ear that might discern my voice. I am again reminded of a memory. When living in Paris while undertaking my study of medicine, I made the acquaintance of a certain gentleman who seemed, to my youthful eyes, extraordinarily ancient. In the morning I would sit near the gates of the Jardin du Luxembourg to enjoy an hour's peaceful contemplation before the day's schedule of lectures, and each morning I would see this man making his way down the Boulevard Saint-Michel. He slumped over his cane in a manner that suggested an inability to stand upright without it. His head remained downturned as well, as though he were watching with the greatest concentration each of his shuffling footsteps. His pace was so slow that I might spend the entire hour observing his progress over a distance that I would traverse in no more than a minute's time.

Finally one morning I approached the man and asked if I might be of any assistance, if I might perform for him whatever daily errand brought him down this street.

"Are you better suited than I for such an errand?" he inquired, without raising his head.

"I am young," I replied, and now the man did move his head upward to regard me.

"Then you are not well suited," he replied, and he smiled at me, not in a taunting manner but warmly. Then he lowered his head and began to shuffle forward.

I was perplexed by his answer but emboldened by his friendly manner. "Might I then accompany you from time to time?" I asked.

"That you might be better equipped for this errand?" the man inquired, and again he looked up at me and smiled.

"That I might be better equipped," I answered.

"Then you may," he said, and thus I began to walk with him in the morning. We did not speak again of what mission took him down this boulevard each day. Instead, I simply listened as he recounted for me his life's adventures, which included sojourns in distant lands that I had only the dimmest notion of where to find upon a map, if at all.

One morning I became so enthralled by his tales that I lingered all morning, neglecting both breakfast and my lectures. It was only then that I discovered that the man's sole aim was to walk down to Boulevard du Montparnasse and then turn around and walk back up Saint-Michel until he returned to his residence.

At his door, he stopped and shook my hand. "Now you are well suited for my errand, Emile," he said. "Please feel free to perform it for me as often as you like."

Now I have become the old man who traverses the same

path again and again, that I might study my own footsteps, that I might know where I have been, that I might remember. That is my sole errand. Thus will I return to my preparations for departing from New Orleans, for seeing John James Audubon again.

That evening I removed my clothing, pulled on my nightshirt, and extinguished the candle, but there was no solace, no consolation in the night. That sleep should overtake me so readily during the day but with such reluctance at night seemed one of age's harshest punishments, at times a greater torment than my palsy and aching limbs. Seated at my desk, I needed only to shut my eyes to fall asleep, but in bed I would lie awake for hours on end, my mind marching forward though my body remained still.

What use was sleep, though, if it would not divide one day from the next? Little comfort is afforded by a morning that gives way to afternoon, an afternoon to evening. I needed to wake to the undefiled light of a new day to feel that I had in some small measure begun my life anew, to convince myself that I had found sufficient cause to undertake the banal though now arduous tasks that awaited me: washing my face, pulling on my clothes, forcing myself to eat and drink though I was frequently without appetite or thirst.

That evening my thoughts traced the whole of the long journey north rather than allowing me to sleep. I saw the carriage's wheels draw their lines in the muddy roadways as I passed through town and wood and hamlet and crowded city. I saw the flickering lights of lodges and inns and taverns, unfamiliar foods stretched out before me as though on a single pine table of immense width and length, the ravaged carcasses of pig and fowl and lamb resting beside toppled bottles and wine-smeared glasses. I saw strangers gorging themselves, the curling smoke of their cigars and pipes, their scarred and unshaven faces. I heard their intemperate humor, their snarling provocations. I smelled the foul odor of their clothing and bodies and breath. I was assailed all around by the lewd and grotesque.

Perhaps I was merely possessed of the fear that the way would be too lengthy, too strenuous, and I would fall ill and find myself confined to bed in some poorly acquitted board-inghouse where I would waste away unattended. But who would attend me in my solitude save the shadowy tormen-tors that possessed my thoughts, that inflamed my suspicion and grief?

Thus I attempted to turn my thoughts toward not the journey itself but the journey's end — when I might stand again beside John James Audubon or lean near him in his bed. Would I be obliged to bend down and put my ear near the man's mouth to understand his words? And would he be sufficiently possessed of his reason that I could comprehend his meaning? Would I find in his words, after thirty years, enough vindication for the grief by which I had been pos-sessed, enough evidence to confirm my suspicion regarding Myra's death?

I remember, of course, the very moment that suspicion was formed. In the early hours of the watch, I held Myra in my arms as though she might provide some comfort to me in my grief. Having observed the fires outside the window and Mr. Audubon's attention to them, I released her, but before stepping away I grasped her hand as if in farewell and by chance noticed the suggestion of a blue tint at the base of her fingernails.

This coloration was not, I was quite certain, a product of rigor mortis (which produces not a blue but an ashen cast to the skin) but instead a symptom I had previously observed in the corpses of women who had sought to attain the frail, gossamer complexion admired by gentlemen by daily and for a lengthy period partaking of *poudre rajeunissante*, which is nothing more than a measure of arsenic suspended in some potable liquid — water or vinegar or wine. This vain and nefarious pursuit had made its way, I had learned in my researches, from Europe to these shores because of the notion, originating with women of peasant stock and unsupported by reason, that consumption of this concoction would add to a woman's natural graces, providing a new and winning luster to her sparkling eyes and bestowing upon her contentment and peace while enhancing her ardent longings for intimacy.

Unlike the prescription of two teaspoonsful of flowers of sulfur in a cup of boiled milk, which a woman might drink before breakfast — a prescription Myra followed until through repeated remonstration I succeeded in convincing her that her beauty needed no improvement — *poudre rajeunissante* is not merely without benefit; it is ultimately noxious, though the small doses by which women ingest the mineral serves to mask its damaging results.

While I had not encountered in my anatomical explorations a victim of intentional poisoning by such means, I reasoned that despite the immediate and catastrophic assault on the body, the very same symptom might present itself in this subtle, nearly undetectable manner if the application of this mineral to the body were of sufficient quantity.

The initial consequence of this observation was a queer euphoria, for here was evidence that Myra had not taken her own life, that it was not despair or dissatisfaction or a dark turn of spirits that had produced her death. I had not failed her, had not been so unfit and unsatisfying a husband that she would choose to end her life.

But the euphoria quickly faded as I concluded that I had indeed failed Myra, for I had not filled my role as her protector by preventing another from doing her this harm. And it was then that my grief took on the peculiar shape that has allowed it to persist so long. Here was an injustice, a crime, and I knew straight away that while I possessed the means to expose its nature, I would not do so because of my own circumstances — for the sake of my own safety. Was I not choosing again, as I had chosen with Lucretia in my youth, my scientific pursuit above all other considerations, over love and justice and truth? Was my position any nobler, any more blameless, than it would be if I had indeed sliced the throats of the thieves whose corpses I possessed?

But there was more. How could I take a knife to Myra's body, so enrapturing and adored, a temple at which I had worshipped and would worship still? How could I make of her a cadaver? No knowledge was worth such defilement.

No knowledge was worth such defilement. Had I not read precisely those words, scowled and laughed and asked Myra to cast them into the fire?

Would I allow another man to perform such an act, to spoil with his scalpel what I could not spoil with my own? I would not. I would indeed place my life in jeopardy to prevent it.

I could not claim innocence, could not assert that I was free of blame, for guilt had again and again fueled my grief. How many bodies had I defiled in such a manner? And I would have given up my own life to prevent the defilement of merely one.

I did not, of course, give up my life. But I had failed to protect Myra, I believed — and believed it still as I struggled to gain even an hour's sleep before my journey.

I had packed my bags, straightened my study, poured myself a brandy. I had paged through Audubon's illustrations, lingered with each of his birds so that it might be imprinted on my memory, so that I might, should my journey reach its conclusion in time, recall the image to him and ask where the bird was found, what behavior was observed, how its pose was determined. I would summon from him a clarity in regard to his work that might instill in him a concomitant clarity in regard to the true subject that prompted my journey.

And was this not to be an act of mercy as well, declaring my allegiance to this man, to his work, distracting his mind for some brief period from the great abyss toward which his body inclined?

I had walked from room to room in my house. I had stepped into each as though there, as at Audubon's bedside, I would pay my final respects. I had removed my clothing, pulled on my nightshirt, extinguished the candle. I had imagined my hands and Audubon's clasped in greeting, my grief swept away.

Not swept away. I am mistaken. *Vindicated.* That is what I sought — vindication, the assurance that I had been right to grieve, to spend my days in fond, inconsolable remembrance. It is by means of memory, I believed, that man is most human but as well possessed of an intimation of divinity, of that timeless state where past and present and future become joined, indistinguishable one from the other.

And then, though I lay there in darkness, I heard with the greatest clarity John James Audubon's voice, though it had to persist like a ceaseless echo through thirty years or traverse the very length of the country to reach me: *what of the bird who travels thousands of miles in migration and then returns across those thousands at winter's end to seek out the very spot where, a year before and through prior years, she built her nest and raised her brood?*

That is not memory, Mr. Audubon, I answered. That is mere sensation, an excitement of certain organs, a mechanical response. Should the bird return and find her nest gone, plucked from its branch by a curious child or the tree cut down by a farmer clearing the woods for his fields, she would perhaps be perplexed, unmoored, but only for a brief period. She would set about building another nest, and when order was restored, this second would take the place of the first.

What of the bird who laments his lost mate, who would sing to her from one season to the next?

Are you certain that the song is a lament, Mr. Audubon? Can you detect in its note the precise nature of the composition? Only a man can understand that what he once possessed has been forever lost; only a man can announce that what is gone cannot, no matter what his efforts, be restored or replaced or reacquired.

I have chosen to grieve these thirty years, Mr. Audubon, for my grief is not merely an illness born of despair. It is also a celebration. It is a shrine, a testimony to my abiding love, an acknowledgment of the divine.

I met Myra, Mr. Audubon, when my youth had already left me, when I had concluded that I would never marry, never see my features reflected in the face of a child. I had just returned from a year in Paris, revisiting the people and places that had been imprinted on my character. While there I sat in the surgical theater's front row, while behind me the young pupils whispered crude jokes regarding the state of the subject under study, their eyes trained less often on the instructor's deft, careful maneuvering of his scalpel than on the corpse's pubis or penis, its sagging breasts or hooked toes. I recognized, of course, that their absurd puns, their raucous laughter, merely disguised their fear. They did not yet understand that only by maintaining the strictest concentration, only by directing one's attention to the task at hand, might one appease one's revulsion and terror at standing over a corpse, cutting it open, eviscerating its arteries and organs. Without such purpose and resolve, the act remains barbaric, inhumane.

Do you attend me now, Mr. Audubon, or have you become a child again, incapable of eyeing the grim specter that looms before you?

Well, we have had this conversation already. Thirty years have passed, but still we remember. In hushed voices, with Myra's body near, we managed to undo the silence that blanketed our grim task. We discussed anatomy, ornithology. We observed by our watch each hour's passage. We recounted our histories and perused the slaves at their labor. We speculated about the Pirries' personal affairs, those of James and Lucretia, of Eliza. We greeted the girl's physician and suitor, my former apprentice, listened to his derision of your character. We awaited the storm's arrival.

Such is our cruel divinity, Mr. Audubon. We are possessed of memories that, given sufficient prodding, will not let go of even the smallest detail — the black orb of an eye, an errant feather, a stilled heart, the blue-tinted crescent at the base of a fingernail.

What did you know of the truth that you did not say? What is it that now, at my journey's end, you must tell me?

You will be forgiven. Thus will I forgive myself.

I must sleep. We must.

And I did finally sleep. My slumber was dreamless and deep, and when I awoke I was unsure, though merely for a moment, whether my journey had been concluded or had yet to begin.

10

Audubon's Birds

Just as I would speak to you, my daughters, though I remained silent so many years, so did Emile Gautreaux finally put aside the silence that attended our watch, as though he could no longer bear the weight of his thoughts. "Mr. Audubon," he said, his gaze remaining directed out the window, his voice as quiet as when he had spoken in secret to his wife. "I am grateful, sir, that you will pass this evening in my company. We had hoped to linger here a while, make your full acquaintance. We had hoped . . ." But his voice faltered.

"You will return directly to New Orleans, then," I said.

"Yes," Gautreaux replied. "Myra's father will of course want to see her." He paused as though he might weep again, but he then continued. "He will want her to have a proper Christian burial. He will want to act quickly, for once he hears of the circumstances, he will fear the church's declaration that she willfully took her own life."

Something in the physician's tone suggested scorn, but I was unsure whether it was directed toward the church or toward his wife's father.

"She did not take her own life," Gautreaux announced, and he looked at me as if to assess in my expression the nature of my response to these words.

"She did not," I said, merely intending to affirm his statement.

"We drank in celebration, Mr. Audubon," he said, his voice rising as though I had countered his assertion. "The occasion was a happy one. We meant only to celebrate our holiday. Nothing more."

"Of course," I responded.

"But I no longer enjoy the favor of the church. For that reason alone, she might be refused a final blessing. Admiral Richardson puts great store in such rituals. He will fear that without a proper Christian burial, her soul will be lost for all eternity."

The man laughed quietly for a moment, looking down at his hands. Then he said, "Such a soul as Myra's cannot be lost."

"No," I said, recalling how I had made the box for you, dear little Lucy, who had hardly a day of health in your two years, and for you as well, my dear sweet Rose, who did not live to see a single blossom of the flower that provided your name. Two hours' carpentry became five on both occasions on account of my great sorrow, and the wood was still stained with my tears when I laid the boxes in the earth — and yours, dear Rose, with blood as well, for the saw slipped in my hands as I cut, and I would not, despite Lucy's insistence, wipe the blood away or apply a bandage to stop its flow. Instead I swore to heaven that I would bleed my own limbs dry to see the breath return to your sweet face. I would to this day swear the same oath, pronounce the same vow for you both.

But though I was lost in my own sorrow, Gautreaux spoke again. "Lucretia," he said, "has anticipated such resistance."

"I'm sorry —" I said, and I wondered if my own face mirrored Gautreaux's grief. "Resistance?"

"From the church," he explained. He lifted his hand and placed it against the window as though he expected to feel there the heat from the Negroes' fires. "Lucretia has summoned the young physician Ira Smith, who can be trusted to respect the circumstance's delicacy. You are familiar with Ira, I assume."

"I am," I said. I had encountered the young physician in his attendance on Eliza Pirrie, though his true purpose seemed to be courting her. His many prescriptions for the girl, whose complaints were as vague as they were frequent, seemed intended more to advance her attachment to him than to restore her health. On one occasion he even insisted that she refrain from all drawing, dancing, and music and occupy herself in quieter, more private pursuits, such as playing a certain game of cards, whose rules only she and her physician understood.

"Though you know him as physician to the Pirrie family and their neighbors," Gautreaux said, "for two years Ira made his residence in New Orleans and was, like young . . . ?"

"Mason," I replied.

"Like young Mason to you," Gautreaux said, "he was my apprentice. He was as well a most able surgeon. While I could hardly endure to carry on when a patient's expression of discomfort reached its highest pitch, Ira's hand remained steady throughout, as though he were standing at some great

distance and the patient's cries were voiced in a language un-
intelligible to his ears."

Such a skill seemed to me indicative of a cruel and com-
passionless spirit, but I merely stated, "It is fortunate indeed
to find so worthy an apprentice."

"Indeed," Gautreaux said, though he frowned. "Ira was,
however, not without his faults. He was, for example, too eager to cast aside true science and embrace the variety of medical theories that have achieved such popularity in our cities.
He would on occasion prescribe Thomson's vegetable distil-
lates and offer readings to certain patients of the thirty-seven
faculties Fowler claims to have identified in the indentations
of the skull." He raised his hand to his own head as if he
would search out the truth of such a claim. "It is absurd," he
said, and he lowered his hand.

Now he looked straight into my eyes. "Just as you, Mr.
Audubon, would object to any depiction that does not reflect
a creature's true appearance and habits, so did I object to Ira
Smith's turning from science to quackery — no matter how
the latter might offer comfort and reassurance which the former cannot. Science, like art, will allow no such distortion.
Its beauty resides in truth."

I merely nodded at this assertion. The throbbing in my
ears had returned, and I considered whether I might now ask
Gautreaux about it. But he waved his arm and said, "I was
sorry nevertheless when Ira's apprenticeship was completed,
for I had grown quite fond of him. His dry English manner
is merely a disguise for a clever and incisive mind and ready
wit. In time, I felt, he would cast aside his flirtation with all
that is dubious and undocumented and return to the true and
worthy tenets of our calling. Lucretia received word, I believe, that though he is attending to an outbreak of the fever,

he will arrive by morning, if not sooner. I will be glad to see him again, though not, of course . . ." Again his voice faltered.

"The fever has, I understand, been quite severe in New Orleans this summer," I said, hoping to prevent Gautreaux from returning to a contemplation of the present circumstances for a few more moments.

"Quite severe, yes," he said, "though I no longer attend to those who suffer. I have become, I'm afraid, more a scientist and teacher than a physician." He looked at me and sighed, as though he felt some regret over this turn in his occupation. "I assume, Mr. Audubon, that you have never found yourself in attendance at an anatomy lesson."

"I have seen the advertisements," I answered.

"And were you at all curious?" Gautreaux asked. He turned away and crossed the room to his wife's body. "Given your own interests, I mean."

"My study is of birds," I said.

"Yes, of course," he answered, nodding. "Your study is of birds. I have long been fond of birds as well. In my youth, it did not occur to me that they might be worth such study."

"There are many who would agree. At times my own wife —" But I stopped, seeing that Gautreaux still nodded, as though attending to his own thoughts.

"I mean no disrespect, but how pleasant it must be," he continued, and his voice rose as though he was unsure either of my hearing or of my attention, "to linger in the air, to make sport with the winged creatures there, to occupy yourself with a feathery catalogue of habitats and migratory paths, with measurements of nest and egg, of bill and talon. How satisfying to depict such delicate forms. That is, I assume, how you occupy yourself?"

Though these words, both in tone and implication, seemed to invite confrontation, I feigned ignorance of such intent, for I would not incite the rage of a man who, I now recognized, was still mad with grief. Our entire conversation circled around the subject of illness and death, even while we stood in the company of a corpse, and that corpse the man's own wife. "It is how I am occupied, yes," I answered.

I watched as Gautreaux pulled his watch from his pocket to inspect the time. He nodded again and returned the instrument to his pocket.

"Were this a bird's corpse," he said, and he raised his hand toward his wife, "you would think nothing of the task before you. You would pluck its feathers. You would cut and fold back the skin to reveal the muscle and bone, which provide the truest display of the creature's form. You would cut through to the stomach to explore its contents." He again turned to me. "You would determine from such inquiry what foods the animal found fit for consumption, which ones it could not digest."

"Yes," I said, the throbbing in my ears growing more pronounced. I stepped back and leaned against the window.

Gautreaux came near, and his eyes shone as though he had been struck by some great plan. "You would fix the animal in some true and convincing pose," he declared, and he assumed the aspect of an eagle, his arms raised, his fingers extended like talons. "You would breathe life back into its form by the skill of your hands."

"That is my aim, of course," I responded, and I began to fear that Gautreaux might strike out as he had done earlier.

"Such actions," he continued, "coarse and bloody though they may be, are the very foundation of your study, are they not?"

"They are," I said, and again he took a step forward.

"They are necessary measures to get at the truth," he said. "You would be accurate. You would know just what to draw. They are necessary, sir. Not merely helpful but necessary."

"Yes," I said, nodding.

"Of course," Gautreaux said, nodding as well, as though he would mimic my every gesture. "Of course." He stepped nearer.

Though the throbbing in my ears continued, I removed my weight from the window and planted my feet, prepared to defend myself from whatever assault might be made on me. The light from the fires outside caught Gautreaux's face, rendering it ghastly.

I cannot fully explain, my daughters, the magnitude of a man's fear when he finds himself in the presence of one who has apparently taken leave of his reason.

But Gautreaux seemed to calm himself then. "You know nothing about my own circumstances?" he said, his voice so quiet that I could hear the Negroes' voices, the snap of the cane as the knives split the stalks.

"I know only that you are a physician," I said.

"During your residence in New Orleans, you knew nothing of me, heard nothing, read nothing?"

"I did not."

"You saw the advertisements, though?"

"I did," I said.

"They were mine," Gautreaux said, and his eyes remained fixed on me.

"I did not realize —"

"And Lucretia? She has told you nothing?" He was whispering now, as though he were afraid of being overheard. "She has not mentioned the difficulties I have encountered, the situation that awaits my return?"

I shook my head, and Gautreaux turned back to face his

wife's body. "Then you should know something of my history, sir," he said, his voice no longer pitched low but oddly gay, as though he had forgotten the circumstances under which he spoke. "At the very least, you might find it" — and again he waved his hand — "a distraction."

Now he motioned to the chairs in the corner of the room. "You should sit down, Mr. Audubon. I'll sit with you. My reason for this visit, besides our taking a holiday, was that I wished to speak with you. I had, though it seems fanciful now, concocted a plan, a proposal. Another occurs to me now, only this very moment, but no matter. Let's sit."

As we walked over to the chairs, I turned to look at the clock that stood against the wall, but of course its pendulum had been stopped in recognition of Myra Gautreaux's death. I thought of my own watch, its stilled hands.

Gautreaux must have observed my glance at the clock, for as he took his seat, he announced, "The day, Mr. Audubon, is just now complete."

For a moment he remained silent. Then he smiled, and I was certain there was madness in his eyes.

"And so my story," he said, but in the brief silence preceding these words, I believed I could hear, somewhere in the distance, a bell marking the hour of midnight.

Though ten thousand days have begun and ended since that evening, I still hear Emile Gautreaux's voice. *Such a soul as Myra's cannot be lost.*

Nor yours, my dear daughters. Nor yours.

II

Gautreaux's History

How shall I transcribe the thoughts that possessed me not only throughout the evening I awaited my journey's commencement but every evening of the journey itself? From one inn to the next, I spoke in silent address to John James Audubon, as though he shared with me my musty blankets and as though I made his sickbed my own.

And so to my story, Mr. Audubon, my thoughts would announce as soon as I extinguished the lamp by my bed. My attempt, of course, was to restore to my own memory the monologue I had presented the evening of our watch, when, accompanied by a pronounced agitation of manner and speech, I attempted to convey my history.

And so to my story, Mr. Audubon, I announced, which I recount neither from vanity nor simply to while away the hours. No, I wish to engage your keener faculties, your logic and reason, so that you are able to discern a greater truth than I can. In short, I seek counsel and instruction. I seek wisdom.

That is where I shall begin, then — with the pursuit of wisdom. How fortunate I have been in my calling. Owing both to my heritage and to my father's considerable wealth, I was able to pursue the study of anatomy abroad. My intention was always to return to these shores to offer to others the benefit of the knowledge I had gained. In Paris, I was obliged not merely to learn the great works of anatomy but to observe and then partake of the very process by which such knowledge is acquired. Like my fellow students, much younger than I, I was asked to step forward, take hold of the scalpel, and learn by investigation and error. As a physician in New Orleans I had performed countless surgeries upon the living, but I had never done so upon a corpse.

Why would this task, of far less consequence and risk than my former actions — when a life had been at stake — seem more challenging, more daunting? Why would this task seem to possess such grandeur, such opportunity for accomplishment?

I spent no little time contemplating such questions, Mr. Audubon, and in time found an answer which must be akin to that which you would provide in regard to your own pursuits. While the physician labors by each of his actions to set right the condition of a single individual, the anatomist improves by his study and investigation the circumstances of the whole of mankind. He must, in all truth, ignore the individual, the eccentric and peculiar and freakish, in order to set his sights on commonality, on the processes and structures of the body.

So invaluable was this training, so transforming the insight it provided, that immediately upon my return I arranged to purchase a suitable building in the Vieux Carré, a small theater that had been home to a French opera company whose great success had prompted construction of a larger venue on St. Charles Avenue, a grand and imposing edifice with which you must be familiar.

You are not? Then I must request that at some later date you join me for an evening's entertainment. Myra cherished such affairs, as women will, and was as intent on gazing from our box to study the habits and fashions of those about us as on turning her attention to the performance below.

The theater I purchased was far more modest. Indeed, the renovations required were minor. I tore away the stage so that those in attendance might look down on the anatomy lesson with a clear view of the proceedings. I did leave in place, I confess, the heavy gold curtains, for I enjoyed the notion of the drama that might be achieved when the curtains were suddenly swept aside to reveal anatomist and subject.

Here was a worthy means of conveying with a single gesture the art that is a necessary accompaniment to science — revelation and enlightenment lying in wait, as it were, for the worthy man with a true thirst for knowledge.

When advertisements regarding my first lecture had been posted and I had invited all of the city's reputable physicians to attend in the company of their apprentices, I stood behind the curtain and heard before me the shuffling of feet, the cacophony of voices, but I was unprepared for what I would encounter when I signaled to one of my pupils, a lanky boy whose name was Lavie, to pull the curtains' ropes. Every one of the theater's seats was occupied. The rear and center aisles were full as well. Even the doorway to the lobby was obstructed, and many other people had yet to gain entrance and struggled to push their way forward to obtain a tolerable view of the proceedings.

I understood then that my audience was not composed solely of physicians and their apprentices, nor even simply of men with a legitimate interest in science. Here as well were the curious and the perverse, those who would find the display and dissection of a corpse an entertainment and who would weave the gruesome details into a gleefully macabre story for a wide-eyed, disbelieving audience in their homes, in taverns, or in the public square. Here too, no doubt, were representatives of the church, if not clergymen themselves, who sought evidence that a man would execute such an unspeakable act, confirming the weekly assertions from the pulpit that man was in his heart capable of every defilement and debasement.

This was not at all what I had envisioned. I had not required payment for admission because I had sought to lure to the theater every physician and apprentice, in the hope that they would come to see the value of dissection, the great knowledge and insight it might offer in our profession. That had been, I now recognized, a terrible mistake. I was alarmed by this turn of events, and, after weeks of anticipation, securing and preparing the body, and organizing my lecture and demonstration, I was disappointed. For I recognized that I could not proceed, could not perform the dissection before such a gathering. The first incision, from throat to pubis, would in all likelihood effect such hysteria, such an outcry, that it would be impossible to carry on. I would have to shout to explain my actions. I would be required to address and answer whatever mockery or contempt my actions met. How could I carve at and break the chest so as to reach the heart? How could I hold that heart in my hands and discuss how morbidity had altered not merely its appearance but the very composition of its tissues?

I could not, Mr. Audubon. I could not proceed. Thus I motioned to the boy Lavie to shut the curtains. When he did not act, I walked nearer to him and spoke, though he could not hear me above the din. I would explain in a moment why the lecture was to be postponed, I shouted, but first he must close the curtains. The body, though draped with a cloth, must be removed from view, concealed.

Lavie now understood and began tugging at the ropes as though ringing a heavy church bell, his thin arms struggling with the task. It was as the curtains' folds finally lurched forward to divide me from the audience, many of whom were now derisively whistling and shouting, that I saw the woman sitting near the front of the theater.

A single woman, Mr. Audubon, among so many men. She sat calmly, her hat in her lap, her gloved hands resting on the edge of the brim. I was struck not so much by her youth and beauty but by her apparent concentration and resolve. Her eyes were trained on me as though she meant to put to full use the knowledge I had planned to but now could not impart. I saw as well how the men who sat next to her leaned away, as if afraid to sit too close to a woman who would freely attend so gruesome a display.

Then the curtains were closed, and the whistling grew louder, the shouting more brazen and vulgar, angry and obscene. I would not, I decided, even step out from behind the curtains to explain, for in doing so I would place myself at bodily risk. I would simply wait for their anger to abate. I would wait until they grew tired of shouting, until they realized that no matter what their entreaties, I would not proceed with the dissection. I turned instead to Lavie and placed my hands on the boy's shoulders. We must remove the body, I explained. The shouting grew louder still, and I declared that it would not do simply to remove the corpse from behind the curtains; we must take it to my home, where it might be kept from public view. Would the boy help me?

He would, he said, so I lifted the body from the table and with Lavie's assistance wrapped the sheet fully around it. We set out through the theater's side door, my arms at the corpse's shoulders, the boy's arms at its knees. "Quickly!" I shouted as we turned the corner and pushed past appalled pedestrians — appalled because, I now perceived, the sheet had slipped and the corpse's head was exposed, the gray pallor of the skin declaring with certainty that here was no invalid but a cadaver.

I quickly pulled at the sheet so that once again it covered the head, and we hurried toward my house. Though I did not look back, I imagined the pounding of feet behind us, imagined the theater's patrons as an angry mob intent on making a full display of its wrath. But were these men angry because I had failed to perform the dissection or because I had proposed to perform it at all? I did not know, and suspected that most did not know themselves. As you are aware, Mr. Audubon, in an animal, the very scent of blood, no matter its source, can provoke a frenzied response. Perhaps men are no different.

We succeeded in reaching my home and carried the corpse to the room upstairs where I perform my private anatomical studies, making notes of my observations and drawing crude sketches, comparing these to the exquisite renderings in the *Corporis Fabrica*. In such a manner I could identify the failings of my own eye and, on rare occasions, the slightest of errors in Vesalius's text.

Having set the body down on the table, I went to the win-

dow and waited for the mob to appear. When it did not, I
sent Lavie home, descended the stairs, and poured myself a
brandy. I then collapsed with exhaustion in my study.

Moments later, however, I heard a knock on my door.
Though I feared that finally the mob had come, I found instead the woman I had seen in the theater.

"Emile Gautreaux?" she said, and she offered her hand.

"Yes," I replied, touching the soft fabric of her glove. Now
I did take note of her beauty, her fine pale skin and delicate
frame, the dark curls of hair beneath her hat. She seemed too
young for the clarity of expression her face had maintained
in the theater. The doubt that now revealed itself in her eyes
seemed truer.

"I had hoped to speak with you after the demonstration,"
she said. "I'm sorry that you were unable to proceed."

"It was impossible. It would have been . . ." And I paused,
unable to articulate my reticence. Had I merely imagined an
antagonism to the demonstration? Perhaps those in attendance possessed a true interest in anatomy. Perhaps their anger was simply caused by my failure to proceed.

"Grotesque," the woman replied.

"Indeed," I said, relieved to have this confirmation of my
assessment.

"Might I come inside a moment?" she asked.

"Yes, of course," I said. "Please." I stepped aside. "I'm
afraid the day's events have left me somewhat flustered.
Please."

"Only for a moment," the woman said, and as she stepped
past me, I directed her to the parlor and waited to sit until
she had taken her seat. She then removed her hat and placed
it on her lap, her hands resting on the brim — the very position she had assumed in the theater.

"I recognize that it is quite unusual —" she began, but she

then stopped and looked directly at me. "Excuse me?" she said.

I was startled. Had I signaled that I was about to speak? Had I looked at her with the same interest and surprise I had felt upon seeing her in the theater? "Your name," I said, smiling, recovering my composure. "You have not told me your name."

"Oh, forgive me. I am sorry. I was a bit afraid . . ." She looked down at her hat. "It is Myra Richardson. My father is Admiral Thomas Richardson."

"I am happy to make your acquaintance, Miss Richardson."

"And I . . ."

"Yes?" I inquired gently, hoping to counter her hesitancy.

"I had hoped to speak with you, as I said. I have an interest, sir."

"In anatomy?" I asked stupidly, for such was my surprise.

"Yes."

"A true interest?" I said, noticing again the delicacy of her beauty, a frailty that might in other women suggest ill health but in this woman conveyed — well, I do not have to provide a description, Mr. Audubon, for here she is, here she remains. "A true interest," I inquired, "not merely a morbid fascination?"

"Yes," she said calmly.

"How would you make such a distinction?" I asked, and she seemed flustered. "I did not mean —" I began, but she raised a hand to me.

"No," she said. "It is a legitimate question, though my answer might seem inadequate." She looked directly into my eyes now, as though she had managed to locate her courage. "I am unconventional. I am not, it seems, like others and have never been so, even from the youngest age, if I am to believe my parents' report." She smiled. She seemed a child still, her skin unblemished, her manner so artless, her assessment of her own character too certain — precisely like a child who declares he will become a statesman or merchant or physician before understanding the true nature of such occupations.

"And your interest in anatomy?" I repeated.

"It is difficult to explain," she answered. "As a young girl, I received instruction that was wholly ordinary. I was particularly adept at drawing, I was told, but I was always dissatisfied with what I observed and reproduced, as if I had not gotten at its true nature, its essence."

I confess, Mr. Audubon, that even this brief conversation had planted a seed in me that would take root and — well, I do not have to speak of love to you, who know full well its bliss. How it must plague you to be separated from your wife, though that separation contains the prospect of reunion.

But to return to my story. Though I might put such a question to you as well, I asked the young woman, Myra, what she meant by her last remark.

"Asked to draw an apple," she responded, "I would split it open and depict its core. Asked to draw a flower, I would uncover its roots. Once, when I was asked to depict my own hand —"

"A common exercise in perspective," I said, remembering my own tutor's assignments and the inept, distorted drawings I had produced.

"Yes," the young woman replied. "But I would, I determined, provide myself a greater challenge, and I hunted among my father's books for one that would reveal what lay beneath the skin. I found such a book and produced a number of drawings depicting the muscles and bones of the hand. My tutor was quite horrified, as was my mother. They expressed concern over the indelicate turn of my imagination, for I was inclined toward melancholy as well. 'So gentle and exquisite a form,' my tutor said, stroking my hand. 'How would you fashion it so monstrously?'

"I was too young, too unschooled, to provide an adequate answer to this question. As for my mother, it was her habit to place my drawings in frames and put them on display, and she seemed vexed particularly by the prospect that I might expect these sketches to hang in the parlor beside the others. 'Do you,' I asked her, 'so lament your child's talents that you would hide them?'" The young woman laughed at the memory, and I joined her.

"I am sorry to say that I did not let the matter drop," she continued. "I teased my mother a bit, suggesting which room might prove best for the display of these works. I announced that I planned to draw the entire body in such a manner. Well, that proved too peculiar and unsettling for her, and she asked my father to speak to me in the library after dinner. She hoped he might uncover a cause for this strange and alarming turn in my character.

"My father, though, slyly professed admiration for my resourcefulness, and he encouraged me to execute further drawings. I kept his book with me and did indeed continue to draw. My fascination did not diminish but increased."

"And the purpose to which this fascination might now be applied?" I asked.

"To your purpose," the young woman said. "To the study of anatomy." She raised a hand to the curls on her forehead. "I would like to be your apprentice."

I could not disguise my surprise at such a request. "Miss

Richardson —" I began, but Myra leaned forward to stop me.

"I understand how others might react to such a circumstance," she said. "But you are not unaccustomed, as I observed this afternoon, to disapproval."

"I am not," I said, and I smiled. "But if I were to take you on as an apprentice, I am quite sure all my other pupils would desert me. Neither science nor my own pursuits would profit from such an exchange."

"You refuse my request, then?" Myra said, nodding as though she had expected precisely this response. She placed her hat on her head and stood.

"I do," I answered, quickly adding, "merely as a matter of reason, not prejudice." But as I looked at her, I understood that I did not wish to have her leave me. Indeed, I would give up every pupil to keep her near. "Miss Richardson," I said. "A moment, please."

She turned to me, unable to disguise her displeasure.

"Miss Richardson, though I too am regarded as unconventional, I must by necessity follow certain conventions, or at least appear to. Thus, although I cannot accept you as my apprentice, I would happily engage you — with adequate payment for your services — as my assistant."

Myra smiled then and rushed toward me to offer her thanks. So moved and delighted was she by my concession that she threw her arms about me in an embrace. But it was I, not she, who nearly swooned.

Thus, Mr. Audubon, did our alliance begin, and within a few months that alliance had deepened to such an extent that I asked for and received her hand in marriage. By then I had discovered the shadowy side of Myra's assertion that she aimed always to get at the essence of things but felt that she had not gone far enough, had not managed to retrieve what lay hidden inside. Her true subject for this pursuit, I soon discovered, was herself. No matter how close her inspection, no matter how honest her assessment of her own character, she felt as though there were some deeper reservoir of feeling, the existence of which filled her with a marked melancholy, indeed with despair.

This would seem, then, sufficient explanation for her death in such a manner. Surely she must have sensed that she had failed and would always fail and thus, in exhaustion and despair, determined that she would drink herself into ruin. You observed her, Mr. Audubon. She would not cease, for look at the joy her inebriation provided. If one glass, one bottle, possessed such power, then her joy might be multiplied by adding a third and fourth.

That is it, then, it would seem. To stave off despair, to keep at bay the dark turn of thoughts by which she was tormented, she would do this. For what greater escape is there than in death?

Yet listen to all I have told you, Mr. Audubon. Did I not suggest that Myra's sole aim was to go beyond appearance to uncover what lay beneath, a truth that might be a far keener measure of circumstances and character than appearance would suggest? Might that not be true here as well?

I do not propose this as a matter of mere speculation, Mr. Audubon. I am certain. Thus I seek your counsel. I ask you to tell me what I cannot see, for I believe — no, I am certain of this as well, Mr. Audubon — that you possess the very same frame of mind as Myra, as myself. You wish to get at the truth in your study of birds. You wish to reveal what has never previously been shown. You wish to find not contentment but true revelation.

What else is here that I do not see, Mr. Audubon? I will answer your every question with candor and completeness, no matter how deeply you probe.

In New Orleans, there may be those who await my return to accuse me not merely of defiling a corpse but of murder. In my possession, in my surgery, are the bodies of three men whom I unearthed, three men whose throats were cut by what appears to have been a physician's knife. The bodies are in my residence. I possess such instruments. I am skilled in their use. Am I a murderer then, Mr. Audubon? Perhaps it is I who took not only these three lives but Myra's life as well.

I will make no further claim upon you, Mr. Audubon, except that you spend this evening in pursuit of the truth. Your study is no more of birds than my study is of corpses. We would get at the truth, Mr. Audubon. We must.

Once my grand and absurd monologue to John James Audubon reached its end and I had at last asked him to divine the truth of Myra's death — only then did I detect the peculiar, ghostly appearance of the man's face, a face somehow familiar, a face that seemed to possess both the sweet innocence of a child in slumber and some dark and loathsome knowledge.

Perhaps I would seem to cast too heavy an authorial hand upon this account if I were to assert, as indeed was the case, that my careful study of the man's face led me to conclude that I was observing not another's features but my very own.

We would get at the truth, Mr. Audubon, I had declared. *We must.* And I saw then, as though I stood before a mirror, my own horror and despair.

12

Audubon's Inquiry

D ear Lucy, dear Rose: The wild thrashing of wings in my ears has become a roar, indescribable in its intensity and the ruin it would cause me. No, my daughters. No. I once encountered such an unholy din in my youthful wanderings. Outside of Louisville, I discovered inside a sycamore of sixty or seventy feet, in the stump of a broken, hollowed branch some forty feet from the ground, the roost of no less than a thousand swallows. I rose early the next morning, long before daylight, and found the tree so I might learn more of the swallows' habits. I leaned my head against the tree, which was utterly silent, and remained in that posture until light began to penetrate the woods, when suddenly I sensed that the tree had begun to fall and would surely crush me.

I leapt away and looked up, astonished to see that the tree still stood. Instead, the swallows poured from the stump in a black stream, the noise of their wings like that of a mill's giant wheel revolving within the rushing torrent of a rain-swollen river. For half an hour they rose like smoke swirling from a chimney, darkening the sky until finally they passed from view, and I fell to the ground then in simple and complete depletion, as though I had come face to face with the devil's dark minions and fought them off with my bare hands and arms.

That, my beloved daughters, is the noise I hear now. That is the exhaustion I feel. I wake to it in the morning, pass my days in its company, seek sleep that I might forget the deafening roar. Your mother attends me still, though she has given up her pretense of happy bustle and sits by my side for an hour each evening, clasping my hand.

I cannot hear the voices about me, nor my own, except in the rare moments, no longer than a few minutes in length, when the roar suddenly quiets. I call to your mother then, though my words are mere wisps of air, a snake's hiss or the dull swish of leaves on a branch, too faint to rise above even the spit of the fire that does nothing to warm me.

Then the cacophony continues. To preserve my reason, I attempt to extract from the din the call of my birds, of Townsend's finch and the black-necked still, of the eider duck and the Florida cormorant, the arctic jaeger and the red-necked grebe, the solitary vireo and the welcome partridge, the great marbled godwit and the black-backed gull, the little night owl and the sora rail.

My study is of birds, I insisted.

No, not of birds. Of truth, Emile Gautreaux said.

He would have me get at the truth of his wife's death, my daughters. He would have me turn from the ornithological to the human. But hadn't I already gotten at the truth, known it the moment I saw that she had drunk herself into an everlasting sleep?

*I will answer your every question with candor and complete-
ness, no matter how deeply you probe.*

So I made a show of my inquiry. I learned the man's full
history, and Myra Richardson's as well. I learned the nature
of her melancholy, her spells of confusion and despair, how
she would retreat to the very house to which I had been invited to draw her figure, at which I had been stirred to such
desire, urged by her toward its fulfillment but then cast out as
though I would challenge her virtue and propel her toward
ruin.

"Did she," I asked Emile Gautreaux, "ever speak of these
spells when they had ceased, when she had returned to her
true character?"

"She did," he answered, pacing about the room, "though
she spoke as though her memory were dim."

"As though her very character had been altered?" I inquired.

"Not altered. No," Gautreaux replied. "Diminished."

"And did she seem so to you?"

"Diminished?" Gautreaux laughed. "How would she be
diminished, Mr. Audubon, if she possessed more of my devotion with each passing hour?"

I recognized, my daughters, the calamitous truth of the
man's words, for I too wished to forget all other intimacies, the countless hours of devout and spirited coupling
that steered your mother and me through our wedded evenings, and remember instead my hands on Myra Gautreaux's
breasts, my lips on her lips, how I clung to her, stirred passion
in her, my lips on her breasts, my hands and mouth descending to explore and taste the warm folds of her sex. Though illicit and profane, never again would I know, I believed, so
fierce an ache and longing, a dalliance that possessed the

grace and recklessness, the sublime wonder, the immeasurable distances of flight.

Would I get at the truth now, my daughters? Would I confess that thirty years later, I cannot provide a contrary answer?

The flight of the swallow-tailed hawk, of the golden eagle. The downy feathers of the white-tailed ptarmigan. The acrobatics of the violet-green swallow. The night-hawk's wings spread out against the burnished sky, the prairie wood-warbler's joyous trill and song. Would I exchange these as well?

Emile Gautreaux spoke to me that evening in quiet reverence of Myra Gautreaux's carnal appetite and how she would call to him and bid him to speak of his desire. *I did not speak*, he said. *I did not speak. I would speak now, that she might hear.*

Again the man wept, at this admission, and stood before his wife's body and clasped her hands in his own.

And I too did not speak.

Then, outside, we heard the Negroes shouting. Gautreaux joined me at the window. The Negroes had stopped their work and stood with their knives lowered at their sides or raised above their heads as though they would defend themselves. The oxen snorted and kicked, their brutish faces shining in the firelight. Something had struck terror among the Negroes, and the oxen sensed this change, as though the air about them had become unsettled, had taken on a new and unfamiliar scent. They strained against their yokes.

I leaned closer to the window, to discover what had stopped the Negroes' work. In the distance, as though he were an apparition invented out of the black night, a man on horseback emerged. The Negroes cowered at his approach. It was the devil himself, they seemed to believe, the devil come to set the fields on fire, to set them all aflame or lead them on a final march to the fiery regions and shadowy air of hell. Many of them fell to their knees. The wind whipped at their torn and mud-streaked clothes.

Is that not the region I now occupy, my daughters? It is as though at any moment I will find as company not you or the gentle creatures of the air but the foul odor of the con-demned, the monstrous roar of the three-headed beast Cer-berus, every scarred soul and forsaken spirit a poet might conjure to convey the torment of the damned.

Would my birds shed their feathers on my behalf, so that I might shape for myself a pair of wings for an airy descent into that dark realm?

I'll see this story done, my daughters.

The horse and rider drew closer. My breath clouded the window, and I raised my hand to wipe it clear. Then I saw that the Negroes had determined with relief, as had I, that here was no ghostly apparition nor the devil himself nor even James Pirrie, who would provoke in them a kindred fear. It was a young man, the physician Ira Smith, come to confirm and certify Myra Gautreaux's death, to assert his authority by inventing the story whereby this woman would remain in the eyes of the church wholly blameless, her soul unsullied.

It was to me that Gautreaux had assigned the task of affixing blame.

Peace to her soul, for my own had turned as black as the evening, as ash.

The golden eagle, my good and fair and loving daughters, clutches a white rabbit's carcass, talons embedded in the head, piercing the rabbit's eye. The white-headed sea eagle stands on the shore over a gutted catfish. The beak of a pere-grine falcon drips with a mallard's blood, the mallard's feathers strewn about him, the mallard's chest gaping. A lifeless vole dangles in the clutches of a sharp-shinned hawk.

Not of birds, Emile Gautreaux declared. *Not of birds. Of truth.*

If he makes this journey, if he is at this very moment on his way, I will hold the demons at bay, withstand the roaring in my ears, turn death a while from my door — so that I might speak, might tell him.

Not of birds. Of truth.

13

Gautreaux's Apprentice

Here, finally, I will turn to the long journey from New Orleans to New York, during which I lost all ability to determine how many days or even weeks had passed. We exchanged our team of horses three times and then four and then five, the Negro Antoine declared, but I was unsure of this as well. The temperature fell day by day as we proceeded north, and wrapped in my blanket inside the carriage but shivering nonetheless, I thought a hundred times that I might call out to Antoine to abandon this absurd quest and turn toward home.

He cannot be alive still, I thought, *nor I much longer.*

But the roads, which at first grew worse, began to improve with each new day; the carriage was not upset; and I had deduced the hand of Providence in my being afforded a companion for my journey. Here too, perhaps, I have been an inadequate author to my tale, for I have waited far too long to provide a fit and timely introduction for one whose role in this story is by no means inconsequential.

My companion was none other than the boy who delivered Lucy Audubon's letter to my door, the one whom I believed — correctly — I spied as I returned home down Royal Street, having made my preparations for departure. The next morning I found him standing outside my house as though he were waiting, his clothes no longer dirty, his nose wiped, the sores on his arms and face no longer open, his feet laced inside a pair of old but newly polished boots.

"Morning, sir," he said as I stepped outside and directed Antoine to retrieve my bags.

I nearly stumbled, such was my surprise at seeing the boy before me again, for I had indeed been visited by a moment of prescience when, observing him running from my door, I had sensed that he would have a further place in my affairs.

"You're going to New York, sir," he announced, and when again I did not reply but merely stood dumbfounded before him, my palsied hand flailing before me, my cane waving in the air as though its copper snake had sprung to life, he continued, "I read your letter. I'm sorry, but it wasn't sealed, sir."

"The letter," I said with an audible exhalation, relieved that the boy's apparent intuition might be rationally explained, though the locus of my surprise merely turned to the fact that he could read at all, so impoverished and untutored had he seemed at our first meeting. I knew then why he stood before me now, dressed in what must have been his Sunday clothes. He wished to travel with me.

"I do," the boy stated, though I was unaware that I had in fact announced my conviction.

"You do?" I said, and the Negro pushed past me, bearing my trunk.

"That's all, Mr. Gautreaux," Antoine declared.

"I've got a great-aunt there, in the city proper," the boy said. "She'd like to take me in." And he produced from his pocket a folded sheet, which he handed to me just as he had handed me Lucy Audubon's letter.

This letter was one of introduction and indeed declared that the boy's great-aunt longed to see him. His full name was Osha Warfield Hansen, she asserted, and hers Belinda Warfield Shepard, widow of one Davis Anthony Shepard, a tradesman. She lacked the means to arrange the visit, but anyone who would consent to bring the child to her would find favor with the Lord, for He had taken the child's parents and sisters from this earth by an awful fire and left the boy orphaned. The letter was dated the third of June, some six months previous.

I looked up at the boy. "Where have you lived since the fire?"

"In the house, sir," the boy answered. "Two rooms were spared."

"And who has cared for you since you were orphaned?" I inquired.

"I care for myself, sir," he said.

"By the wage earned as a messenger?" I asked.

"And by selling what remained in the house that wasn't ruined. But I've sold off everything now, and I'll soon be taken to the Catholic home, unless . . ." The boy regarded me.

"How old are you, Osha?" I asked, leaning upon my cane, for my legs ached from the previous afternoon's errands.

"Fourteen, sir," the boy replied.

"And you wish to travel with me?"

"I do, sir," he said.

"It is a long way," I cautioned, and I regarded him sternly, so that he might understand my full meaning. "I am an old man. If I should take ill in the course of the journey, you would be returned here. Antoine must return you."

"I know, sir," he said.

"And you have no one here, no family at all?"

"None, sir," he replied. "They all went in the fire."

"But you did not."

"I jumped from the window, sir. I broke my arm, I think, but it's healed now. I can lift anything. I'm strong. And I'm not afraid."

"Of the journey?" I asked, and the boy looked down at his feet a moment but then returned my gaze.

"Of you, sir," the boy said. "Postmaster says I ought to be. He says you dig up bodies. He says you're a doctor and you cut into them or you used to. I said I didn't care. I said I wasn't afraid of such a man."

"Why aren't you afraid?" I asked, smiling now, fully aware that an extraordinary circumstance had come to pass.

"I don't know, sir. I'm just not."

I thought of my first encounter with Myra, how she had professed no fear of my pursuit of anatomy, how she had merely attributed her interest to her peculiar character, to her desire to peer beyond appearance.

"What would you make of yourself?" I asked him.

"I don't know, sir. I'm a messenger, though I can shoe a horse as well. And I can read and write."

I was reminded of the young boys who came to me, their fathers standing behind them and nudging them forward, boys who asked if they might serve an apprenticeship, explaining that they had been schooled by the Jesuits and wished to become physicians.

"When might you be prepared to set off?" I said.

"I'm ready to go this moment, sir," the boy replied. "I've got my bag." He pointed to a canvas duffel, a mailbag, behind the carriage.

"Then I've no choice," I declared, and I turned to Antoine and asked him to place the boy's bag on the carriage.

"I knew you'd take me," the boy said, smiling. He slapped his hand against his leg. "I said you would. Postmaster owes me a dollar now, but you'll have to get it for me when you return."

"I will indeed," I replied, and I laughed then, though I knew that while Providence may have delivered to me this companion, it was unlikely to deliver me home again.

In this way I came to keep watch over Osha throughout the days and weeks of the journey, though in all truth he did more to watch over me. He was, I soon discovered, a child of rare intelligence — his father and mother were both schoolteachers, he said — and he was possessed of inexhaustible good spirits. I am quite certain that if not for his presence, I would have abandoned the journey. It became my conviction, in fact, that the reason for Osha's appearance was to insure that I did not turn back, for in doing so I not merely would have abandoned my prospect of reaching Mr. Audubon in time, which was in any case a doubtful one, but would have prevented the child from reaching the one person on this earth who would care for him.

As for the Negro Antoine, he and Osha became quite fond of each other as well, sharing the reins so that we could make swifter progress than a single driver could have managed on his own. At the inns where we rested, Osha often joined me in the bed, and while he thrashed about in his sleep as the young will do, he warmed the blankets with his youthful vigor.

Thus did I, a man who had lived so long in solitude and seclusion, find myself in the company of one who restored my spirits by his very presence, who attested that despite the tragedy he had endured, he would find renewal.

The journey was indeed a long one, and I soon determined that if I were to falter and grow ill, unable to carry on, I would not command Antoine and Osha to turn back but would send them on without me, for surely the boy's journey promised far greater rewards than my own.

One morning, when a cold rainfall was slowing our progress, Osha came down from the bench and swung himself inside the carriage and asked if I would tell him the full reason for my journey, for I had done little but provide a vague explanation of my purpose. Though I knew that good and moral judgment would forbid me to convey to a child of fourteen years many aspects of the story, I felt as well the need to speak of those matters that for so long had occupied my thoughts.

As it turned out, Osha's interest in the story was primarily confined to two matters — first to my suspicion that Myra had been murdered, which propelled his imagination toward countless conjectures regarding the true nature of each person's character, and second, to my former apprentice Ira Smith and his affection for Eliza Pirrie. I return now to Ira's appearance, which I have yet to recount.

I observed the surprise on Mr. Audubon's face as he peered out the window. "Your apprentice has arrived," he said, and he wiped his hand at the glass. "The Negroes were startled by his horse."

"Would you see him inside, Mr. Audubon?" I requested, and he was unable to disguise his pleasure that he might have a moment's relief from our watch. I feared that in conveying my history and asking him to get at the truth of Myra's death, I had done little except persuade him that I had lost my hold on reason.

"Of course," he replied, and he quickly stepped toward the door. Again I turned to the window. Outside, the Negroes had returned to work. If they had been startled by the horse's approach, it was perhaps because they had imagined it bore James Pirrie, who would move about them, stirring them by his voice or his crop to quicken their labor. Other than a strong wind, there was still no sign of a storm, though Mr. Audubon had suggested that James had expressed in his letter complete certainty regarding its course.

I was unsure how much I should reveal to Ira Smith about Myra's death. When he had served as my apprentice, my faith and confidence in him could not have been more profound, yet I wondered what alliances he had forged as a result of his admiration of Eliza Pirrie, who despite her youth seemed no more a child to me than Lucretia, as both of them possessed an aspect to their character that would allow them, given enough prompting, to act in opposition to morality as well as good judgment.

But for what cause would either have sought Myra's death? Might Lucretia, given her unhappy union to James, have clung so long to the sting of our parting that she would strike out at me through Myra? Such a notion seemed absurd — and it was more absurd to imagine her daughter possessed of such evil intent.

Who, then, would strike at Myra so secretly, with such skill and planning that she would be poisoned by her drink?

Only I would have such knowledge and foresight. Only I. And now I did seem, even to myself, stripped of my reason, for even knowing my own innocence, I accused myself.

Then the door opened and Ira Smith stepped inside, with Mr. Audubon behind him. Ira embraced me warmly, with true feeling, and I found myself comforted by his presence.

"I'm terribly sorry, Emile," he said. "It was quite a shock to receive such news."

"Yes," I answered. "Yes. I'm afraid I have not yet fully recovered."

"Nor should you," he replied, and he embraced me again.

"You seem well," I said.

"I am well," he replied, "though this is a trying summer. The fever is doing its work throughout the parish and well north, though surely it must be far worse in New Orleans."

"It is," I answered, and I looked beyond Ira to Mr. Audubon, who remained by the door as though he were a schoolboy waiting to be excused. "I understand that you are acquainted with Mr. Audubon," I said, and Ira turned to regard him.

"I am," he announced. "Both Mrs. Pirrie and Miss Pirrie have sung his praises so loudly that all would have cause to know of Mr. Audubon throughout the parish."

"And beyond," I said, "for it was Lucretia who spurred our interest in him. I am afraid the artist possesses a charm among women which we physicians do not."

Mr. Audubon remained silent but bowed as though made truly uncomfortable by such open praise.

"Why would it be, Mr. Audubon," Ira inquired, "that the artist would gain such favor? Is it that women put great stock in what pleases the eye, and while your work would pursue beauty at all costs, our own would pursue —"

"Truth," I interrupted, detecting a taunt in Ira's question. Mr. Audubon was clearly aware of it, brushing at his shirt and rocking from side to side in agitation, as though prepared for the escalation of whatever feud divided them. "Mr. Audubon and I, Ira, were just speaking of such matters. We concluded, I believe, that our pursuits are not so different after all. Both would make truth their aim."

"Then Mr. Audubon's charm must have another source," Ira said, and he turned away from Mr. Audubon in what appeared to be impatience and disdain.

Mr. Audubon stepped forward and said, "I will leave you a while to your unfortunate business. I will return at the hour's end." And he opened the door and left the room.

"I am sorry, Emile," Ira said. "I should not have made a show of my . . . vexation. This is no occasion for ill feelings."

"What prompts them?" I asked, though I knew from Mr. Audubon that they had found themselves in competition for the attention, if not the affection, of Miss Pirrie.

"His entire character," Ira answered. "He is, I believe, wholly without restraint." He turned toward Myra and then back to me. "I'm terribly sorry, Emile."

"No," I said. "I have an interest in Mr. Audubon. In what matter does he lack restraint?"

"In all matters," Ira said, walking to the window and looking out. "You may know," he continued, "that Miss Pirrie and I are to be married."

"I knew of your inclination, Ira," I answered, "but I did not know of this happy development." I went to him and shook his hand. "I'm pleased. She is a beautiful and winning young woman."

"And Mr. Audubon, as I have well learned, has an eye for such beauty," he said. "Lizzie has told me of no fewer than a dozen occasions when Mr. Audubon's actions were designed to foster an intimacy and candor beyond all propriety."

I intended to answer this accusation by asserting that perhaps Mr. Audubon's general enthusiasm and candor had prompted Miss Pirrie to misinterpret her tutor's actions, but at that moment the windows and walls began to shake as though they had been seized in the grasp of a giant. The Negroes shouted, and the sky flashed with lightning.

The storm had arrived — and not with a gentle, escalating rain but with the full force of a mighty typhoon. Ira and I looked out and saw what seemed more a tableau vivant, an act of theatrical invention, than a true vision. Mr. Audubon stood before the Negroes, his arms raised in the air, the Negroes gathered around him, shouting and pointing, the rain quickly extinguishing the fires whose light had accompanied them in their labor. Then all together, as though Mr. Audubon were their general and they a vast and obedient infantry, they began to run, heading toward the muddy hill that led down to the low house but disappearing from view as the storm quenched the last of the fires.

"He is a fool," Ira muttered, but I detected that his true response was far different from the one he announced, and as lightning and thunder cracked and roared in the dark skies outside and once again shook the walls and windows, I turned in panic and anxiety to look again at Myra, to offer her the soothing words she would solicit from me, as she had on many prior occasions, to quell her fear of so forceful and magnificent a storm.

It is absurd to suggest what I saw then, for who would believe such a story — that her features now seemed to convey neither fear nor the tranquillity of sleep but a fierce, indeed uncontainable scorn?

For whom? I asked in silence. *For whom?*

14

Audubon's Devotion

How much longer, my beloved daughters, can I endure the darkness that has descended on me? How much longer can you abide my joyless company? If only you could summon your mother here to see you as I see you now, despite this darkness. She would marvel at your beauty, weep with joy to hold your delicate hands, touch your bright cheeks. She would place her lips to your hair, embrace you, whisper in your ear as I would whisper now, proclaiming her love and mine as well.

My voice is nearly gone, but do I require a voice for you to hear? This bed has become a storm-swept boat and the floor beneath, the swirling waves. My body is tossed forward and back like that of a child in a cradle. Will the ground open and present an abyss that might engulf myself and all around me?

Oh, I will finish soon, my dear girls. I want you to know that in the storm which struck so quickly and with such ruinous intent, I thought my life would end in the water, in a flood that would remove every brick and plank and tree and creature of Oakley plantation. I spoke to your mother then, my sweet daughters, as I speak to you now.

Dear Lucy, I said in silence, and I want you to hear my words now so you might understand how even then I sought your mother's forgiveness.

Dear Lucy, though you and the boys remain a thousand miles distant, though I lack paper and pen and could not, if I spoke aloud, hear my words above the din of the rain against the roof and walls of the low house, I will speak to you nevertheless, sending my words into the storm as though carried aloft by passenger pigeon or blue-headed dove or by the currents of the wind itself, a soothing music by which to wake you gently and remind you of my great regard and true affection.

I am huddled now among a hundred or more Negroes, men, women, and children whom I have led from the storm in a frightful panic. We have taken refuge in the blazing heat of the low house, for the Negroes' dwellings will not survive the brunt of the storm nor even, in all likelihood, its early assault, which we now endure. I would take them indoors and allow them to haunt the rooms of Oakley house, but they would surely waken Lucretia Pirrie and she would no doubt see them all whipped directly — directly, I should say, after showing me the door.

The widower Gautreaux, whose wife has taken her own life through drink and now lies on a table in Oakley's parlor, was to be my companion throughout the night, or I was to be his, but I have left him in the company of his former apprentice, who is physician now to Eliza Pirrie, my student. You have heard nothing of this in my letters, I know, but merely this single day's incidents — though it now be the morrow — are beyond easy summary and, it would seem, all logic and reason. It is enough to say that the storm within Oakley house is as alarming and possessed of ruinous intent as the storm without.

As for my student, the Miss Pirrie of whom I have written to you, I am quite convinced that nature has not heretofore known such a perplexing and contradictory creature, unless it be the wolf, which once grown shies from all human company but when young is as easily and reliably tamed as the whelp of any domesticated bitch, which — the wolf, I mean — one moment might pounce on a darting hare and tear into the bloody carcass with ravenous appetite but the next moment take a scare from the twitching of a squirrel's tail. The wolf will howl in hellish, piercing tones to proclaim its dominion, then whimper at the briefest separation from its mate.

So the young Miss Pirrie, who at any given moment carries within her diminutive form more secrets, more strange and unholy ruminations, more quick turns of mood and spirit than most would exhibit in a lifetime. Am I puzzled by a girl of such tender years? Indeed I am, though I make no apologies, for he who was not puzzled might be deemed a simpleton. Are all women so complex? Not you, my great friend and helpmate. Your every action speaks of your unwavering love and great devotion.

Dear Lucy, if I might offer evidence of my own devotion, I would recount the explicit temptations this young woman has time and again contrived to place before me. Gone unremarked but not unnoticed are the occasions when, declaring herself at a loss, she has asked me to place my hand over her own to guide it through some simple exercise, her left hand reaching up to my shoulder as if to steady herself but moving then to my hair, her fingers becoming a gentle comb.

I have felt the warmth of her body pressed ever more firmly against my own as I have attempted to steer her through a simple waltz. Certain that Joseph's gaze has been directed toward the piano in his futile effort to produce a discernible melody, she has allowed her legs to become entangled with my own, so that I have been left no choice but to enclose her in my arms to prevent her from falling to the floor.

"Thank you, John James," she whispered on one such occasion, as though breathless. "I am clumsy, aren't I?" And these words were followed by a brief but unmistakably ardent embrace. We continued the lesson, and when she insured that she would stumble again, I pretended distraction and allowed her to fall. She looked up at me from the floor, her eyes alight with both anger and shame — here too the eyes of a wolf who has feasted on a meal that was not his own. She understood that this was no accident, that I understood her attempt to snare me in a further embrace and my distraction was a ruse by which I might offer her further instruction.

Joseph stopped his playing to rush over and assist Eliza to her feet. His exclamations of concern were so exaggerated as to make clear to the girl what he had already expressed to me in private — that he believes himself in love with her. She blushed at his attentions, straightened her dress, and then left the room. The happy result of this episode is that she has become, in our subsequent lessons, a most accomplished and graceful dancer. She has not stumbled again.

Even so, the girl's mother claims that I solicit her daughter's affections, I scheme to rob the girl of her virtue. I would not tell Lucretia Pirrie that I cannot steal what has already been given freely — not to me, dear Lucy, but to Ira Smith, the girl's physician. One evening a few weeks ago I could not sleep and happened to stand before the window, for I'd heard an owl's call. There I happened to witness, in much the manner I witnessed it this evening, the young physician's approach. I went downstairs to greet him, but before I reached the door I heard outdoors the voice of Eliza Pirrie, though I could not discern her words nor those of her suitor.

But such is my loneliness in your absence that I would offer speculation. Did they speak of love as I would to you, of how the hours and days lengthen when they are apart? Did Eliza find some honest expression of her attachment, or did she perform for this young man a maddening, flirtatious dance of feeling, a dance he would be content to witness for its fleeting moments of pleasure — a kiss, a tender word, a smile, an embrace?

I returned to my room but heard, though less distinctly, the sound of steps upon the stairs, the gentle closing of a door. And though I would undertake any enterprise to rid myself of such thoughts, to stop my ears, I could not prevent my mind from drawing, as though it would guide my hand on the page, a depiction of their secret drama, their every action and gesture all the more extreme on account of my sleepless solitude. Thus their passion was in my thoughts rendered grand and desperate. He would take her in his arms. She would allow her nightdress to slip to the floor. He would raise his hands to her breasts, caress their nipples. He would part her thighs. What words would pass between them now, or does he move against her, inside her, in silence, in ardent worship or deliberate violence? Does she meet his approach with a stifled cry?

Oh Lucy, my dear wife, would that you and I were engaged in such a demonstration of our desire, our embraces unhurried, our every pleasure sanctified. We would twine our limbs, call out even now our wild surprise, a union affirming our holy bond.

But my thoughts cannot remain in such a sweet realm, for death seems all about me. The Negroes are swooning in fear and exhaustion; mothers are searching out their children in the crush of bodies as though we were aboard a slave ship making its passage in rough seas. I think of my father, his figure not frail with age but fully possessed of its youth. He rocks and sways before me, and I see him lie down. I see him reach for the one who lies near him. It is my mother, I know, but I cannot discern her features, for my father lies across her, her head beneath his shoulder, her eyes closed. She is still and silent; then she is calling out, though he would muffle her cries. Is this joy or anguish? I have lost, it would seem, all ability to make such determinations. Am I filled with desire or with loathing?

Then my father weeps. He stands, lifts a child from my mother's arms, pulls the sheet over her breasts and shoulders and finally her mouth and eyes and forehead. He weeps while the child in his arms kicks and reaches out and cries.

I will speak, Lucy, though you will never hear these words. Have I not time and again proven my character? Why is it then that this one night seems to pose a greater threat to my soul than any prior occasion? How is it that I feel myself put on display, the Negroes' eyes turned to me as though I might calm the storm, Emile Gautreaux in his grief asserting that his wife could not have died by her own hand, charging me to uncover some further cause so that he might find a mark for his great anger at this loss?

All men would choose anger over grief, for in the former

we are predator, while in the latter we are prey. We are simple beasts, then, dear Lucy, and I am no better than other men. When my thoughts turn, as they will again and again, to our daughters' fate, I possess such fury that I would curse the very heavens and wring the neck of any man who dared to step across my path. I would take delight in the dull thud of a mortal blow, would laugh with derision at the flow of blood, the hollow gasp of a final breath. All so that I might not grieve, dear Lucy.

I speak these words in full knowledge that if you were truly able to hear my voice, I would be silent, concealing the barbarity and turmoil that reside within.

I am the cause, dear Lucy, of this woman's death. I have forsaken you, forsaken myself. I am possessed of such rage that I would take my rifle in hand and aim it toward the heavens. I have brought this night on my own head. It is my own soul, my own heart, that has been forever darkened.

I would train my rifle on the most delicate and beautiful of creatures, the ruby-throated hummingbird, the mangrove cuckoo, the summer redbird and scarlet tanager. I would steal the life from each to assuage my affliction, to show how such grief can find fit display.

I have lost too many. I would find them all.

This storm rages and cries out and thunders like none I have previously encountered.

As do I for you, for your forgiveness.

As I do for you now, my beloved daughters, who would hear my story's end before the storm engulfs this bed, before I am swallowed, alone and pale, in the great abyss below.

15

Gautreaux's Approach

I n his innocence, the boy Osha moved from one conclusion to the next regarding the truth about Myra's death. With each new chapter of the story, he felt certain that he had brought to light that which had previously been hidden. He believed he knew who had committed the crime. It was Lucretia, he claimed one moment, who must have poisoned Myra's glass, hoping to win my affection. No, he said the next, it was James Pirrie, for wasn't he the one who dispatched the wine we carried in our carriage? It was he, Osha cried out, though he had meant the poison for his wife and none other, that he might be free of his repellent bond.

But I drank as well, I asserted.

"Not so fully, sir, you've said," Osha countered. "Would the arsenic be like water? It can be cold or warm or even hot and leave you fine, but if it's scalding, then one touch will leave its mark."

It might, I allowed, and I was struck once more by the

boy's intelligence, his precocious powers of analysis and observation. He had listened to my story with great concentration, his hands fluttering in the air as I spoke, as though he would formulate and then solve an equation.

He wished to hear as well about my travels abroad, journeys more protracted and harrowing than the one we now endured. He wanted to hear of Florence and Venice, of Rome and Vienna, of Paris and Madrid. He yearned for stories of the surgeons Astley Cooper and John Hunter, of Abernathy, Bell, and Munro, of their countless midnight excursions and my own to secure fresh specimens for study. Our dangerous escapes, our fear and folly, were to the boy endlessly fascinating, as though I were merely concocting a frightening tale so that the woods about us would seem populated with chilling phantoms and ghouls, which would relieve the dreary monotony of our swaying carriage.

He found the same fearful pleasure in Keats's *Hyperion*, which I read to him when my mind was dull with approaching sleep and I could not continue with my own tale. *Every man whose soul is not a clod,* the poet declared, *hath visions, and would speak, if he had lov'd,* and Osha nodded as though he understood, as though he imagined the poet spoke of me.

He wished to hear of Myra and bid me return time and again to our fated meeting, when she asked to learn the anatomist's profession, to stand at my side so that she might always do my bidding and I do hers, so that we might make light of those who would do us harm, curse our names, put to an end the progress of science.

And Osha returned as well to his speculations, for despite his youth, he understood that here was the single question that had held my attention for thirty years.

Perhaps it was one of the Negroes, he asserted, a Negro

recently flogged and hoping to repay James Pirrie for his cruelty. Might not that Negro have applied the poison to the
bottle? Or perhaps Eliza Pirrie, on account of some persis-
tent quarrel — perhaps she wished to be free to marry her
young physician. Perhaps she had meant the poison for her
mother. Or what of the young physician himself? Osha inquired.

He was not there. He could not have done it, I might have asserted but did not. I would not declare to him that telling
this story had made me grow most suspicious not of another
but of myself, and perhaps I had for thirty years borne a futile
grudge. How could I have announced so lamentable an error
after our journey had gone on so long — thirty years of re-
lentless brooding and speculation whose only answer was the
madness of grief?

Thus did my story become little more than a grim amusement to distract us from the cold, which penetrated the carriage and crept beneath the blankets. Our every breath was
written in the air; our fingers and toes were numb. We endured a heavy snowfall, a storm of sleet and ice; the roadway
turned into a muddy swamp, and trees fell across our path.

Antoine, I believed, was sick with a fever, but he would
not come down, for he said the temperature had fallen so
much that it was no longer safe for the boy to drive. He was
as fine a Negro as I had met, and I announced to him that his
reward at our journey's end would be his freedom. I had dispatched a letter to New Orleans to this effect, asking the
bank to pay twice what his master deemed his worth, three
times that amount if the man resisted. No doubt it was this
prospect that kept Antoine at the reins, so great is every
man's desire to be free of his shackles.

As was my own.

I did not speak of such matters to Osha, for he was too young to know the truth behind my tale. My shackles, my grief and despair and suspicion, had seemed their tightest when, at the Pirries' plantation, with the storm still raging outside, I led Ira Smith to Myra's body. I could not speak but took hold of her hand so that he might detect on his own the blue tint to her nails. If he spoke, if he ascertained this symptom himself, the matter would be beyond my powers, I silently declared. He might demand further investigation. He might offer to open the body himself, request an official inquiry. It would be his doing.

But instead he hardly looked at Myra. He placed his hand gently on my shoulder and assured me that he would make a record of her death that would allow no insult to her character or to my own. And that was all. He waited, paying a silent tribute to her, perhaps uttering a prayer, and then he remarked on his exhaustion and bid me to attempt sleep as well upon Mr. Audubon's return.

"Should I summon him?" Ira inquired. "He could keep watch a few hours while you slept."

"The storm is too severe for you to go out," I said, for indeed we now had to raise our voices merely to hear each other. "You should remain inside, Ira, and sleep. I am sure Mr. Audubon will return once the Negroes are settled and the storm abates."

Thus Ira did leave me alone with Myra, and so great was my torment that I thought then I might find some means to end my own life and take my place beside her. Surely that would produce the very inquiry for which I hoped, though its only foreseeable conclusion was that I would be deemed as frail of mind as Myra had been when she drank herself to this fate. Or perhaps everyone would conclude that I had, in my desperate misery, taken her life first and then my own.

My mind turned to the bodies of the three thieves that awaited my return to New Orleans, and I knew that with Myra's death I had lost not only her company but all desire to study anatomy. I might never again look upon a corpse without having my thoughts turn to her. How sweet indeed did John James Audubon's pursuits seem to me at that moment. I would not find Myra's form in the feathers and muscles and skeletons of such creatures. None would be affronted by such study. None would declare me a lunatic, the devil's servant, a scourge. None would burn my figure in effigy, calling for my flailed corpse to be tied to the stake, so that strips of my charred flesh could be sold to those whose fathers and mothers and uncles and brothers had been subjected to my demonic and merciless knife, my hair turned into a mourning brooch though none would mourn my fate, my eyes torn from their sockets, my testicles cut from their sac, my skull set atop a fence post, my bones boiled for lime, my heart left in the street for consumption by buzzards and rats and flies and maggots, the very memory of me, of all I had once hoped to learn and accomplish and impart, swept away, obliterated, by Myra's death.

I screamed in terror at this imagined fate and screamed again in rage and horror and anguish. My screams were so loud that they rose above the storm and woke Lucretia Pirrie and her daughter, summoned Ira from his preparations for sleep, called out — though surely this could not have been the case — across the smoldering fields to John James Audubon and lured him away from the huddled Negroes, called as well to James Pirrie upon his mount riding behind the storm, following its ruin, so that all might return to witness my final debasement and undoing, the gold ribbon at Myra's waist undone, her dress torn from neck to pubis, my hands clawing at her breasts and abdomen so I might tear her open, show all who would dare uncover their eyes this final blood-smeared and irrevocable truth.

No, I did not tear and claw at Myra. I called out and in time was surrounded by the other inhabitants of the house. And before them, I simply fell to my knees and wept. Did I know even then that I might be mistaken? Did I weep not merely for Myra but for the madness that had overtaken me?

As I was engaged in the recollection of this final act of madness and despair, Antoine called down from outside the carriage and the horses quickened their pace. "We're approaching the city of New York, Mr. Gautreaux," Antoine cried. "Look ahead, sir. Look ahead now, Osha. I can surely see it."

16

Audubon's Vision

They are all about me now, my daughters. First came the rose-breasted grosbeak. Did you hear him, dear Lucy, dear Rose? He woke me from sleep with his serenade, a song so rich and mellow in the night's stillness that sleep fled from my eyes. Next was an owl, an Acadian. He too was charmed by the delightful music and thus maintained a reverent silence. Next to join these two was a blue jay, who brought with him a husk of corn, which he now places between his feet and hammers at with his bill until he has split the grain and picked out the kernel.

Now Bewick's wren stands on my chest and hops sideways, with its head first toward me and then turned away, and a wounded flycatching-warbler is perched on my bedpost, its tail spread and wings opened, snapping its bill again and again to keep me away. A Carolina wren circles my head and then alights there, drooping its tail and singing with great energy a brief ditty. *Come to me, come to me!* it seems to cry, so loud and shrill yet agreeable that I would join its song.

Do you not see what I see, hear what I hear?

Look now. Harlan's buzzard has come to rest at the foot of this bed, its bill a pale blue though black toward its end, its mouth a yellowish green, its iris a yellowed brown, its feet a dull green, its claws fully black, its plumage compact, a deep chocolate brown. Here are a ground finch and a common crow, a purple gallinule, a great blue heron, a tufted puffin, a horn-billed guillemot.

Here is a woodthrush. Many a time, my beloved daughters, have I fallen to my knees on hearing his melodies and there prayed earnestly to our God.

And as I raise my hand, palm open, a ruby-throated hummingbird descends, its throat glowing with a fiery hue, its body a resplendent changing green. Who might witness this creature moving through the air, suspended as if by magic, its motions supremely graceful, a glittering fragment of the rainbow — who would not by the hummingbird's very presence turn his mind with reverence toward the Almighty Creator, the wonders of whose hand we encounter at every step?

If only another of this species perched on my other hand, for the feelings displayed by a pair of these creatures provide ample instruction in the true mechanics of love, as does your sweet presence, dear Lucy and Rose. But see how the male swells his plumage and throat and, dancing on the wing, whirls around and around his companion, dives toward a flower, returns with nourishment that he will share. How full of ecstasy he is when his gentle caresses are kindly received, when his sincerity and fidelity and courage are so entirely admired that the result is a pair of tiny hatchlings, naked and feeble and blind.

It is these hatchlings I most resemble now. Beneath these stale blankets I am naked, so feeble that even the hummingbird on my hand proves too weighty. And now, though I know each of the birds about me, know their calls and twitterings, the varied impressions left on my skin by beak and claw and talon, I am blind.

I call to your mother and ask her to brush away the birds from my chest and hair, for they make each breath a mighty struggle.

"We are alone here, John James," she says, and I am sorry that she, possessed still of her eyes' use, cannot share my wondrous vision. I would tell her that we are not alone, that every moment another of my birds flies through the open window, takes its place where it will, cries out its wonder, its very signature, each feather a quill with which it might transcribe on the page its features, each feather sharpened so that it might cut its own carcass open, revealing esophagus and thorax, stomach and sternum, muscle and brain and heart.

"Our daughters," I say. "They are here too." But your mother turns away to hide her tears.

"I have found them all," I tell her, though I am not certain she hears me above the birds' calls, above the thrashing of their wings, above the rush and torrent of the river as it overflows its banks and spills toward us, above the roaring winds of the ever-strengthening storm.

We were all there, I would tell her, like the birds in this room: Emile Gautreaux, Lucretia Pirrie, her daughter Eliza, her husband James, the Negro Percy announcing that he had finished the box, the physician Ira Smith, who kept his eyes trained on me, my young apprentice, Joseph Mason, who, like me, averted his eyes from the corpse.

And I, dear Lucy, dear Rose. And the storm raged still, though its winds, having wreaked their full damage, now merely tore through the limbs of trees already fallen, through windows whose glass had already been shattered, through the splintered boards of the Negroes' collapsed quarters. James Pirrie's books had been thrown from their shelves, his maps spilled from the drawers of overturned cabinets, though I could not say if this was the work of the storm or of Emile Gautreaux in his fury, for he had torn his wife's dress from her and draped it about his shoulders like a ceremonial banner.

Who, Mr. Audubon? Who? he shouted, and though all about me expressed alarm that the man's grief had caused him this greater affliction, I alone knew his meaning, I alone understood that he had become possessed not by madness but by the torment and anguish of the victim, of one who has been rendered blind and therefore must flail his arms about to clear a path and know all that stands around him.

Thus we observed his apparent undoing. James Pirrie turned away, peered out the window, and cursed the storm's ruin of his cane fields.

"They are not ruined, James," Lucretia announced, her voice stern and dismissive, as though she would spit the words at her husband. "I have saved them."

The man glared at her in disbelief, and I understood then, my dear girls, what I should have recognized before. I understood that though James Pirrie had indeed dispatched a letter warning of the storm, it was Lucretia Pirrie who, by an act of forgery in her room after reading the letter, had appended to the first page a second. Thus had the ink smudged on O'Connor's thumb, and thus had O'Connor cursed the irrational and premature conclusion that the cane should be cut though it seemed too young. The irony that attended this circumstance, I discerned, was as darkly comic as the act was vengeful. Having intended to cause the cane's ruin, to chide and then expel her husband for his inattention and infidelity, his cruel fits of inebriation and immoral swaggering, she had instead managed to save the cane, to steal profit from impending loss. Even nature's mighty brawn and wrath had met its match in Lucretia Pirrie's scorn.

How might I fare, then, now that I had lost favor with this woman? Would I, on behalf of my birds, cling to my quiet retreat and paradise at Bayou Sara and preserve my place in this wretched family?

Who, Mr. Audubon? Who? Emile Gautreaux shouted, and I might have said at least that there had been true deception here, though not of the sort Gautreaux imagined.

But I said nothing.

And the Negro Percy announced again that the box was done and would be brought up straight away once the rain and wind had ceased. And Ira Smith embraced Eliza Pirrie, whispered into her ear some word of comfort or perhaps a mocking assertion regarding my character, while Emile Gautreaux stood before his wife's body and called out again, *Who, Mr. Audubon? Who?*

All turned to me then, but I would not answer.

Regard his expression, Emile Gautreaux said then, strutting about the room as though he were a character on the stage. *Regard his expression and say you do not detect there knowledge. Say you do not observe some truth beyond the common man's understanding. Say you do not perceive the very depths of his discernment and comprehension. Say all this, and I will declare the matter done.*

No one answered, though Emile Gautreaux halted before them. He eyed James Pirrie, then shook the man's hand. He leaned toward Lucretia and kissed her cheek. He bowed to Eliza Pirrie, wrapped his arms about Ira Smith. He thanked Percy for his labor and nodded toward Joseph Mason, who stood near the door, frightened.

Then he turned to me, and I met his gaze. "Might we speak alone, Mr. Audubon?" he asked. "We have passed this evening together. I would not have it end in this way."

I nodded my consent, and Gautreaux looked to Lucretia Pirrie, who directed the others out the door, approached Gautreaux, and embraced him. "We will be near, Emile. Simply call out," she said, and then she left.

Gautreaux walked slowly to the window, my daughters, and stared outside as though he would study the destruction. "The storm has ended," he said, and when I joined him at the window, I saw that it was true. The rain had ceased, the winds had quieted. The promise of light rested on the horizon beyond the ravaged woods. All was silent outdoors save the rushing waters of the Mississippi.

All was silent, and I threw open the window. I sensed in the air some great catastrophe, greater even than the events that had transpired in this room, a calamity that had yet to reach its conclusion.

Then I understood: for the first time in the weeks that I had made my home here, the approaching dawn was not accompanied by birdsong. How many, I wondered, had been taken down, as though by an able marksman? A thousand? A hundred thousand? More than any man could count, though he spent a lifetime at this task?

It was then that the birds first took roost inside me, my girls. The plumed partridge and pinnated grouse, the duskey duck and loggerhead shrike, the night-hawk and wood-wren. How vainglorious and unknowing my pursuit had been. How inconsequential. How devoid of true understanding and sympathy and grace.

Now the birds seemed ripped out of the sky, not merely from the woods about me but from the whole of the earth. I would not get at the truth. I would evade it.

Thus the birds, gone from view, began to fly toward me. They would pierce my skin, feast on my organs, penetrate the leathery hide of my heart, so that they might drink and, by drinking, give me life again.

It is loss, it is great agony, that gave me my birds, just as that agony has given you both to me now. How great and wonderful a gift, that I might paint in the blackness of a bird's eye my mother's death, my abandonment at so young an age, when I still reached for my mother's breast but found my arms and mouth and stomach empty. There you are in that eye. There is my soul's eternal restlessness, the dark spirits that reside within me and force me to leave your mother and brothers to wander through every region, every wood and field, every summit and valley and shore, to make this vast country my own.

I would find them all.

Listen, my daughters, and you will hear of an act of the greatest mercy, the Creator's sublime forgiveness. Listen and you will hear what I heard in that dawn of thirty years ago, at some distance but distinctly: a bird's call.

"She is gone," Emile Gautreaux whispered beside me, and he lowered his head, closed his eyes, and wept.

I reached into my pocket, pulled out my watch, that worthless trifle, and placed it gently into the man's hands. "The hands have stopped their movement," I said. "The engine is stilled. I give it to you now in remembrance, aware that its use to you might be only to mark this sad evening."

Though he did not open his eyes, though I left him there at the window weeping, I saw that Emile Gautreaux held tightly to the watch, as though he would never release his grip on it.

17

Gautreaux's Answer

Yes, I had believed the world bereft of miracles. I had believed in science, in nothing, in my own grief. But how would I, how would any man, cling to doubt, having witnessed my success at reaching my journey's end?

But even more: for thirty years I trailed Myra's ghost with a persistence and devotion surpassing even that of John James Audubon in pursuit of his birds, a blind and futile hunt fueled by my anguish. What would I have said if I had found in my mad searching that this elusive ghost of Myra had finally turned to me, peered with longing into my eyes, and heard my words? Would I have declared that indeed this was sufficient, that I had spoken and been heard, that truly one soul had understood that my life was not one of cruelty but compassion, how my aim was not to profane but to exalt?

You might conclude that, having found Audubon still alive in his bed, having pieced together his testimony from the shards of memory that cut through his dementia, I would deem these thirty years squandered. Was I not finally in the company of a man whose life, like my own, had reached its final turn, a man whose vision and reason and sublime art had been stolen from him by time, though he would hold them forever in his grasp? Was not this man, from whom I had expected to find vindication for my despair and grief and suspicion, instead the one who showed me that my life might be declared only ruin and waste?

But I cry out now not in anguish but with joy. I declare my every remaining breath precious.

Listen. Though the journey seemed by all measures both tedious and futile, once its end was near at hand, finding Audubon's residence proved effortless. He was well known to all about the region — as I was once known, though not so charitably, within my own — and we were directed to trace the river's course nine miles north of the city, where we would find the estate bearing the name Minnie's Land, upon which stood the great artist's home.

"Is he alive still?" I inquired of one man whom we hailed.

The man shook his head and peered up the road as though he might see through all the miles ahead and divine an answer. "He keeps inside," he finally said, "and has for a long while. Some say that though his body remains, his mind's long perished. I see Lucy from time to time. She seems well." The man shaded his eyes to see inside the carriage. "Are you calling as a friend?"

"A physician," I answered, and I thanked him.

I informed Osha that I would ask Antoine to steer the carriage toward his great-aunt's residence in the city before I proceeded to my destination, but Osha's features suddenly lost their luster.

"You wish to meet Mr. Audubon?" I asked him, raising my good hand to his shoulder.

"I'd be honored to meet him," Osha answered, "but it's not that, Mr. Emile."

I waited, but the boy turned away to look outside.

"You would hear Mr. Audubon's answer?" I inquired. "You would find out what he might know regarding Myra's death?"

"I would, sir, but . . ." And still he kept his eyes from me.

"I have spoken to you freely, Osha," I said. "Speak as freely to me now."

He turned to me, his eyes red, his nose streaming as it had the afternoon he handed me Lucy Audubon's letter.

"I'd like to return with you to New Orleans, sir," he said. "I have to."

"But your aunt," I objected. "Her letter. She would —"

"My aunt's not there, sir," Osha said, and he cowered before me as though expecting to receive a blow, as though I held my cane high in the air before him as I had done when we first met. "My aunt's dead. She's been dead some time now."

I called out to Antoine to halt the carriage and kept my eyes trained on the boy. "I do not understand, Osha," I said. "You gave me her letter. You sought passage."

"I'm sorry, sir," the boy said, and though he was then silent, his eyes seemed to plead for forgiveness.

"The letter was a forgery, a fraud?" I said quietly. "The whole matter was a deception?"

He shook his head. "It wasn't, sir. I had another letter shortly after. From a neighbor, a friend. It said she'd died. It said I ought to know so I wouldn't seek her out."

"But you did," I said, confused and troubled. "You did seek passage."

"I did," he said, and again he turned away.

"With what intent, Osha?" I took hold of the boy's shoulder and made him turn back to me. "With what intent? Theft?"

He looked at me, his eyes unblinking, but he remained silent.

"Murder?" I said. "You would murder me as well?"

Again he did not speak, and though it caused him no little surprise, I called out to Antoine that he should continue on.

"Where will you take me, sir?" Osha asked, his voice wavering, his body shivering.

"To Mr. Audubon," I said, and I laughed. "To Mr. Audubon. I would not deny you my story's end. And I would not be denied your own."

"I don't understand, sir," he said, and though I might have told him my thoughts, I did not, for I would not humiliate the boy. In the course of our journey, he might have stolen from me a thousand times but had not. Any evening he might have taken my life while I slept. Though he perhaps determined that he lacked the courage for so terrible an act, I recognized that it was not a matter of courage nor, of course, of mere curiosity concerning Myra's death. No, here was a boy who, in the end, must see the truth win out — not in my story but in his own heart.

"I don't understand, sir," he said again, and I offered my hand to him.

"Let us find Mr. Audubon first," I declared. "Then we will attend to the issue of your fate."

I turned then to look out the window. Though late in the month of January and thus in winter's bitter grip, this day was promising to be unseasonably warm, the sky blue and clear, the snow-covered banks of the Hudson glistening, reflecting the sun's light as though bright diamonds were embedded there.

Antoine allowed the horses a leisurely pace, as though he

hoped to insure that they would not falter before we reached our destination.

"Look here," I said to Osha. I removed John James Audubon's watch from my pocket and placed it in his hands. "Study this, and I will finish my story — rather, I will bring it as near its end as it can be brought."

He took the watch, and I spoke to him now not with restraint, as I had previously done, but freely.

The Negro Percy and Audubon, I explained, placed Myra in the box Percy had constructed, and they carried the box outdoors and set it into the bed of a carriage. I followed them and took my place, gripped the reins, and, once James Pirrie had stepped clear of the horses, drove away. The muddy lane of Oakley was strewn with fallen leaves and branches. Many of the great oaks that lined the lane were split, their roots exposed and their trunks leaning northward as if still caught in a savage wind.

When I pulled Audubon's watch from my pocket and saw that its life had been restored, I decided that surely there could be no beneficent power that would follow our lives' course, for what God or Creator would use His magic to restore this worthless instrument to life but would not apply such fantastic skill to someone so precious and adored? If this world is one of miracles, why not those that would arrest the deepest sorrow or correct some bold and despicable injustice?

Thus I kept Audubon's watch throughout the years, not as a reminder of Myra's dear life or how I mourned her death but as a declaration of the great void, the infinite emptiness, that lay beyond the clouds and sky.

What then were these birds to which John James Audubon would devote his life, in which I had perceived such promise and grandeur? Was it not merely the notion that as they sailed so high above, they would draw nearer the divine presence residing there? Was it not that their flight would invest them with a sublime transcendence? But without such a presence, what would these creatures be? They would seem no better to our eyes, no more graceful, than the tunneling worm who leaves his dull design in the black soil.

What then was man, if there was no divine being in whose image he had been fashioned? What was our life's work if it would only preserve the lie that we would pave the way for some finer, more blessed existence?

And what was Myra, now that her life had quit her? A corpse, a cadaver, a banquet for the tunneling worm, a subject for the anatomist's grim and pointless study, lips and breast and pubis possessed not of some ethereal and enticing power but merely of flesh and tissue and blood.

Thus would I keep Audubon's watch with me, that I might place my hand against its face and feel the engine's movement and know that I would pass each hour in unflinching despair, the pointless miracle of its movement a testimony to the wretched truth of a world where time marches forward, one moment to the next, though it holds no promise of redemption. Why had I lived so long? Why, I inquired of Osha, had he been spared in the fire that took his family?

Osha did not answer, but his expression clearly displayed his confusion and doubt.

"Here we are," I said as the carriage halted before Audubon's estate. "I will see if Mr. Audubon has our answer."

"He is blind," Lucy Audubon announced as she invited me inside. Her back was bent by age, her hair white as the snow we'd seen on the banks of the Hudson. She greeted me at the door warmly, though she confessed that she had only the dimmest memory of dispatching the letter I presented. Leaving Antoine and Osha to see to the horses, I stepped inside and told her of the letter's contents, for I was unsure that in her frailty she could make out her own words. I explained that her husband had spent an evening keeping me company upon my wife's sudden death thirty years ago.

"He wished to speak with me, you wrote," I told Lucy Audubon. "He wished to convey a confidence that would provide me some comfort."

"He will not, I'm afraid, be able to offer you much comfort," she declared, though she led me through the house.

"I wish to see him nonetheless," I replied.

"Yes," she answered, somewhat wearily, as though any number of visitors had asked merely to set eyes upon her husband and pay their respects.

"He hears, I believe," she said quietly as we reached the door to his bedroom, "but he may not decipher your meaning. He speaks as if to himself and sometimes will not speak at all for hours on end. He asks at times for his daughters, though they passed away as infants. I am afraid, Mr. Gautreaux, that you are likely to conclude that your long journey will have been in vain."

"I would, Mrs. Audubon, if it is no great inconvenience, like to see him nonetheless."

"Yes, of course," she replied, and she opened the door. "I will leave you with him. He is asleep but should wake if you speak a few words."

"I do not wish to wake him," I said, backing away, but the kind woman put her hand on my arm and smiled.

"Then you might wait another day or more," she said. "He requires wakening. It will do him no harm."

She did leave me then, closing the door behind her, and I approached Audubon in his bed. Here, no matter the whiteness of his beard and hair, no matter the gaunt frame and ravaged skin, was the young man I had encountered thirty years earlier. He was possessed still of the features he had possessed then — the angular jaw, the stately forehead, the feminine brow, features that attested to the man's confidence and regal bearing but as well to a fragile temperament.

"Mr. Audubon," I whispered, but he did not stir.

"Mr. Audubon," I said again, louder now. "It is Emile Gautreaux, physician of New Orleans."

His eyes opened, though he did not turn to me, having no use now for his eyes.

"Victor?" he said. "John?"

"It is Emile Gautreaux of New Orleans." I leaned nearer and rested a hand on his arm. "You asked me to come. You wished to speak with me, you said."

"You are mad as thunder, John, you say, but I am madder still. Whose hands have made these? Whose hands?"

"Mr. Audubon," I said. "I am Emile Gautreaux. I was friend to the Pirries, by whom you were employed. James and Lucretia Pirrie. You served as tutor to their daughter. My wife — you kept watch with me, sir. Do you remember?"

Audubon coughed quietly, without force, and closed his eyes again as if to sleep. How little room, I considered, would there be in this man's memory for a single evening thirty years ago? He had traveled throughout the world, produced in his *Birds of America* an incomparable work. Yet he wished to speak to me, he had said.

"It is Emile Gautreaux. I am Emile Gautreaux of New Orleans," I declared again, gently gripping his arm to wrest him from his lethargy. "I am Emile Gautreaux. You wished to speak to me, you said. You would ask my forgiveness."

"Forgiveness," Audubon muttered, though his eyes remained shut. I was elated that he might signal that he had heard my words, that he knew of the circumstances of which I spoke.

"My forgiveness, sir. You would ask my forgiveness. You kept watch with me through the night. There was a storm. My wife —"

"A storm," Audubon said. "My birds." He raised his hands from the bed as though he would reach toward me. "You have seen my birds?"

"I have seen them, sir," I answered. "I admired your birds and admire them still. I am Emile Gautreaux of New Orleans. Thirty years ago —"

"Thirty years ago," Audubon said. "Thirty years ago." I began to despair of ever reaching this man. He would merely mimic my words like a parrot.

"Thirty years ago —" I began, but Audubon raised his hands again, as if to silence me.

"Thirty years ago," he said, "I watched a physician weep."

"Yes," I cried out. "That was me, sir. I would weep now that you remember."

"I remember," he said, and his eyes opened, and I saw clearly the gray film that covered both pupil and iris, the eyes' lens discolored and hardened by cataracts, a condition that had resulted in his blindness but one that I knew could be corrected. In Paris I had observed the oculist Daviel perform such an operation on a dozen occasions, though I had never done so myself.

Should I tell him of this diagnosis? Though he might live no more than a week or even a day beyond such surgery, would he wish his sight restored? What would he care to see? The birds outdoors?

"Do you remember, Mr. Audubon, the occasion of my weeping? My wife, Myra —"

"I remember," he said. "I drew her."

"No," I said. "She died and you kept me company in my watch." I leaned nearer and spoke quickly, so his thoughts would not be steered off course. "I asked you to consider the circumstances of her death. I asked you to turn your inquiry from the ornithological to the human, to discern the true cause of her death."

"I drew her," he said again.

"No," I cried out, again gripping his arm.

"I drew her in New Orleans," he announced. "In the Faubourg Marigny."

Had he indeed drawn her? Would not Myra have mentioned this? "Yes," I said quietly. "She had a house there to which she —"

"I did not know her name."

"Myra," I replied. "Myra Richardson Gautreaux. You were in St. Francisville, at the home of the Pirries."

"She possessed a rare beauty," he said.

"Yes," I answered.

"I drew her portrait, drew her figure."

"You wished to speak to me of her death," I replied.

"Why would I speak of death?" he said, and he quietly laughed, his arm waving slowly in the air as though he would show me this room. "It is all about me."

"But your wife," I replied. "Your wife sent me a letter. You would ask my forgiveness."

"I would," he replied, and again his eyes closed. He coughed.

"Mr. Audubon," I said, raising my voice now, despairing again that I might ever succeed in prompting sufficient lu-

cidity in his speech. He had drawn Myra, he had said. He
had drawn her. On what occasion? At whose behest?

"I pray that you listen to me now," I said. "I have come
from New Orleans to speak with you, to learn from you what
you knew but failed to tell of on the evening of Myra's death.
For thirty years I have mourned my loss. For thirty years I
believed I would never know how Myra met her end. I believed she was poisoned, though I did not know by whom
nor for what reason. I am not sure I believe it any longer, sir,
though I can provide no greater evidence for this conclusion
than I might for the first one. But I have come here to inquire if you possess any knowledge to help me see her life
and thus my own with some measure of certainty and peace.
For thirty years I would not acknowledge that she may have
died from her own despair, that she would choose to leave
me. Do you understand my mission, Mr. Audubon? Do you
attend my words?"

"I do," he answered. "My mind is not in ruins." He
coughed again, and his body shuddered. He opened and
closed his eyes. "My words are slow," he said, and again he
coughed. "They are ill formed, but there is reason in them."

"I am sorry, sir," I replied. "Please forgive my impatience."

"No," he said. "Do speak. I will listen. Your life."

"My life . . ." I began, but I did not know what I might say
beyond what I had already declared. He might speak, if he
had the strength to do so, for hours and hours. He might tell
of his adventures, speak of his good fortune, discuss his endless quest on behalf of his art, in pursuit of his birds. But
what had my own travels shown me? What had I learned? I
could not speak.

Instead I reached into my pocket and removed the watch.

"I have with me," I said, "a gift you presented to me. Now

that my life is almost done, I wish to return it." I took Audubon's hand and placed the watch in it.

"A watch?" he said, holding it gently, for he could not maneuver his fingers.

"Your watch, sir," I answered.

"My watch," he said, and here was no question. He remembered. "It was useless. Vanity and fancy led me to purchase it. I should not have given it —"

"It works, sir," I declared, "and has worked since the day I last saw you."

Audubon seemed to attempt a smile but again began coughing. I took the watch from his hand and held it to his ear so he could discern the truth of my words.

"Do you hear its engine?" I asked.

Now he did smile, and I returned the watch to his hand. "So the years have passed after all," he said.

"They have," I answered, and I smiled as well.

"I thought perhaps they would not," he said. "But we have grown old."

"We have," I said.

"And while the watch works, we will grow older still with each swing of the hands."

"Yes," I answered.

"Our affliction is the same, then," he said.

"It is," I replied.

"And our life's work as well, as I remember," he said.

"No," I said. "I gave up my study of anatomy after Myra's death. You pursued your art and made —"

"Truth," he said. "I believe that is what you told me, was it not?"

"It was," I answered.

"What truth did you uncover?" he asked.

"None. I abandoned —"

"Nor I," Audubon said. He turned his head from side to side. "Do you hear them as well? They're all about me now."

"I'm sorry?" I replied.

"My birds," he said, and he raised the hand in which the watch rested. "They're all about me."

"Yes," I said. I understood that though this claim seemed a delusion, it was not. Would not I, if I had continued my study of anatomy, find myself surrounded by all the bodies on which I had worked? Instead, there was but one, that of Myra.

"I don't understand them. They squawk and cry out and even speak, but I don't understand them." He paused as if to listen to their cries, but then, as though he had heard my thoughts, he said, "You have kept your wife with you."

"Yes," I said.

"Is she here now?" he asked. "Is it she who has led you this far?"

"Your letter —" I began to say, but of course I understood his meaning. "She is here," I said.

"Then it is to her I should speak," he said. "It is from her I should request forgiveness. Do you believe that I would be forgiven, Mr. Gautreaux? Do you believe she would understand that I meant no harm, that I merely admired her beauty, that I was —"

I would not have him continue, though. I did not wish him to name whatever intimacies had passed between them. "Did you indeed draw her?" I asked. "Did she ask you to draw her?"

"Yes," he replied.

"And this drawing?" I asked. "Did you present it to her?"

"I did not," he said. "I destroyed it."

"Why?" I asked.

"It announced my desire," he said. "I was ashamed."

"Of your desire, or of its representation?"

"I do not know," he said, and he turned his head away. "I do not know."

"Then we are the same," I announced, and I took the man's hand again and held it. Did I know whether the loss of Myra had caused me to grieve so long or whether that grief had risen from my innate melancholy and despair? Was it my own character that had again and again given life to that ghost, just as Audubon seemed still to do as well, as though he would carry his vision of her until his final breath?

"I have never known how to speak of them," Audubon now said. "I thought that I might. I thought that I might tell you."

"You have told me enough," I said.

"I had no choice," Audubon said. "I had no choice." Then he pushed himself up a moment, but he sank down again. "I wish that I could say more," he said, his voice growing fainter. "That your journey might end better."

"No," I answered, and we remained quiet, for we had concluded whatever business there had been between us. I would, I knew, ask nothing more of him. And in the silence of this room, I thought not of Myra but of the boy Osha outside. What would I tell him of what had occurred? How could I speak of it? What words might I say to craft a fit conclusion?

I would keep him at my side. I would, if I were granted another year on earth, retrace my own life's course. I would, if he would follow me, as I believed he would, take him to Paris, to London, so that he might learn all he wished to know and pursue without worry, with every advantage, whatever path his fortune placed before him. Perhaps his own story might be triumphant, as Mr. Audubon's had been, no matter his frailty.

Audubon spoke then, as if he knew that my thoughts had turned to him. "There," he whispered, "out that window. There, though I cannot see it, a raven spreads his glossy wings and tail and sails onward. Do you see it?"

"I do not," I said.

"Go then," he said. "Stand at the window."

I rose and moved to the window and looked out across Audubon's estate — at his slumbering orchard, at the hill gently sloping down to the Hudson. At the road, I could see Antoine and Osha on the carriage.

"He rises higher and higher with each bold sweep," Audubon said, as though he could indeed see what he described. "But see how he aims to convince his mate of the fervor and constancy of his affection. See how he gently glides beneath her. They sing. Do you hear their song?"

"It is your gift, not mine, to hear them," I said.

"No. Listen," he said, "and you will hear them as well." He grew silent, his head inclined to the side. Then he spoke again. "They sing to each other, back and forth. Their tones are joyous. Listen. There is as well a melancholy strain."

And here was a miracle indeed, for as I listened I believed I could hear, though at some great distance, the song that Audubon had conjured. "I hear," I said. "I do hear them."

"Attend to them," he said, his words growing still fainter. "They recall the pleasure of their youthful days. They recount the events of their life together. They live again all their sorrows and find strength in their singing. Do you hear them?"

"I do," I said, and though I knew Audubon would now

hear only his immortal birds and not my mortal voice, I spoke to attend to such words myself, words to counter the sad poet who had seemed for so long to speak on my behalf.

"The laden heart's burden," I said, hearing my own voice now, not the poet's. "Its burden is eased, not made weightier, by meeting another heart sick with the same bruise."

Thus was my own burden lifted. Thus had I found my answer — in my own voice, from my own mouth — and thus I left John James Audubon to attend to his birds' every call, that we might both learn, in our own manner, how we would be guided beyond this world to another realm.